Kasauli Lights

Kasauli Lights

Dimpy Ajrawat
Vinny Ajrawat

PARTRIDGE
A Penguin Random House Company

ISBN: Hardcover   978-1-4828-3758-2
           Softcover   978-1-4828-3757-5
           eBook   978-1-4828-3756-8

To order additional copies of this book, contact
Partridge India
000 800 10062 62
orders.india@partridgepublishing.com

www.partridgepublishing.com/india

Acknowledgements

'The spectator ofttimes sees more than the gamester,' says Thomas Hood. How true!

With humble and contrite hearts, we thank our respective spouses Sukhvinder and Sweety, who lost a few springs of nuptial companionship to a long span of our busy solitude since the conception of Kasauli Lights.

The expense paid, to help this project see the light, was not the pulse of genius but the consistent approbation and critical appreciation of our mentors, Mr. Sushil Goel, Mr. Madan Lal, Mr. Arvinder Singh, who have been the pillars of our motivation, our colleagues Gaurav Goel, Karan Goel, Saurabh Goel, Varun Goel, and friends Boparai, Jatinder, Kamal, Sharad, Sukhwant, Samridh, Christina, and Vandana Jain.

We also have to express gratitude to dear Winky, Kuldip, Raju, Daisy, Gurpreet, Sonia, Rimpy, and Harpinder as they preferred to stand fast in our faith.

Milan, Aparjit, Komal, Ridaiy, Armaan, and Ishaan afforded us the realization of our dream as they reconciled with our absence, at times, when they needed us by their side.

We are extremely thankful to Mr. Ajay Arora, Capital Book Store Chandigarh, who rendered invaluable guidance. A special word for Dolly and Pankaj for their inputs.

Thanks to the woody aromas and pleasant breezes of the small little wondrous colonial town of Kasauli, a summery refuge to the literary icon like Khushwant Singh, as it facilitated our stream of creativity.

Immense aesthetic appeal was rendered to the cover page by the creative ingenuity of Rajan of Mindspan.

We would like to thank our publisher, Partridge India, a Penguin Random House company, who showed confidence in the debutantes, its editors who helped make the text flawless.

We also acknowledge the diverse strengths of each other that complemented so aptly to provide existence to this book.

No words but as much gratitude as the seas of the world can absorb for our parents and the creator, God almighty. Prayers of the former did it all.

Last but not the least, thank you readers for picking up Kasauli Lights and being a part of our dream.

Kasauli of My Dreams

Kasauli, as if a dream has a face,
A face, I perceive, I delight in.

On its far-off, well-lit peaks,
Sit the blissful skies,
Changing colours from blues to greys,
Pouring moist on lids I raise,
Satiating my hungry eyes,
That's all I long for.

On its far-off dusky peaks,
Dwells a cottage charming and old,
By the voiced pinewoods shivering in cold.
Just there;
A crackle in hearth, a story in leaves,
A hand that warms as I read,
Caresses me, a gaze with a passionate weave,
That's all I long for.

On its far-off nightly peaks,
Live those little lights, dim, pale, bright and sleek,
Just then;
Gentle on my spirits when sorrows climb,
Dissolve in ecstasies in cheers sublime,
Comforter in disguise, when world gets worldly,
Light up my hopes when fears come swirling.
That's all I long for.

Kasauli, as if a dream has a face,
A face, I perceive, I delight in.

There is no pain time cannot dilute . . . Seek and actualise the reasons of your existence, coded in these four riddles . . .

Gypsy speaks

Chapter 1

The Mystic Riddles

It was late evening on 17 April 2012 when I bumped into Manvi again at Indira Gandhi International Airport, New Delhi.

I was flying to Mexico via Miami by American Airlines to represent my company in a fair to be held in the city of Guadalajara. Being a cautious flier, I had checked in early enough and had a couple of hours' time on hand before boarding. As a routine, I shopped for a bestseller at a bookshop in the swanky Terminal 3 building and settled down to read it in the lounge with a cup of coffee latte.

Maybe it was her beautiful white top that caught my eye or was it her vivacious voice ordering for a cuppa that resonated in me? I so dearly wanted that vague silhouette to be hers. My heart missed a beat as she turned around. Manvi, who otherwise had a figure to die for, was today wearing a black wraparound to keep herself comfortable on the flight. A Louis Vuitton handbag and those big glasses made her look very cute. The act of trying to balance her coffee, muffins, handbag, and carry-on in her usual clumsy style only added to her spontaneous charm even further.

With wheels under feet, I reached to her rescue.

"Hi, Manvi," I said, taking hold of her stuff and guiding her to my table. Having sufficiently recovered from her juggling act, she piled everything on the table and gave me a big bear hug.

"Hi! So nice to see you again, Ashwin," she responded to my greetings cheerfully.

I was admiring the curls which were falling on her right cheek, just the way I loved them, when she teasingly asked me, "Are you done with your inspection, Ashwin? And if you are, tell me where are you off to?"

Before I could hunt for an excuse to camouflage my embarrassment, she continued, "I am going to Mexico City to cover an event being organised by Confederation of Indian Industries."

I could barely believe my ears when I heard this. "Oh wow! I am also going to Mexico to take part in an exhibition," I blurted out.

I surreptitiously looked at her belongings to see if I could spot her boarding card. Perhaps, she could sense my anxiety and started looking for it too. Her demeanour changed from pleasant to anxious to almost hysterical when she got up and sprang back towards the coffee counter, with the ever-loyal me in hot pursuit, just like a pug following his master in a TV commercial.

The boarding pass, in all its majesty, was lying on the coffee counter. Obscured by the mugs, it must have remained invisible to the barista.

To her big relief and my vast dismay, she collected her trophy and marched back triumphantly. I too walked back but slower and slackened, more like a freshly punctured football.

"Typically me," she said, colour returned to her cheeks as it drained out of mine.

"What's wrong?" she quizzed when she saw me going a little pale.

In the meantime, I was gathering my wits which had almost abandoned me. I put up a brave face, although I was feeling quite low and said, "Nothing".

I did not have the courage to tell her that my castle, as recent as two minutes, had been washed out by her 'Emirates boarding pass' tsunami. What could have been an access to highly classified information about her seat number had no relevance now.

The initial tides having settled down, I asked, "Will you be staying in Dubai or do you have a connecting flight?"

"I will be in Dubai for only three hours before I catch a connecting flight to Mexico City. Are you on the same flight?" she asked in a very straightforward tone.

I could not find any anxiety in her voice. Since I had just gone through the complete gamut of these emotions, I presumed I had become some sort of an expert on judging them. I took a deep breath, the Indian yogic solution to such minor heart attacks, and said, "I am flying to Miami and then onwards to Guadalajara. I would be in Mexico for about a week." The changing frequencies of my vocal chords, surely a giveaway, allowed me only that much liberty to keep my voice straight.

As we settled down and sipped our coffee, my senses calmed down to normal. She had always had that kind of hypnotic binding on me which I could rationally classify into attraction. Whatever it was, I had always enjoyed her presence and this time, it was no different.

"Where did you vanish on the afternoon of *Holi*?" she quizzed with a glint in her eyes.

The word *Holi* brought a rush of memories. Samar's image came haunting back to me. Samar, a handsome, rich businessman from Chandigarh, was my bête noire in matters of the heart. I kept quiet for a moment and countered, "Why did you disappear from Bhuj so suddenly?"

She smiled and said, "Work."

She finished her coffee while I silently admired the curls falling on her face.

"Do you know, Samar is already in Mexico on a holiday? I am planning to meet him the coming weekend, and we have planned a trip to Tequila on Sunday," she softly let out a shocker for me.

This was a news hard to digest. The excitement on her face had a disastrous effect on my state of comfort.

"Why don't you join us?" she asked.

"Actually, my travel plans are already fixed," I answered her, not entirely truly, like somebody who had been vanquished in love.

Perhaps she could sense my feelings as she tactfully changed the topic and proceeded to teach me a few greetings in Spanish language, which presumably she had picked up from the Net. Thereafter, she counselled me about the various delicacies available in Mexican food as I continued to focus on the movement of her hands which I found to be very charming. Only once, I nodded my head as she mentioned my favourite dish, the chicken quesadilla. By now I was almost ready to write a poem on her persona when I heard the pre-boarding announcement about my flight.

I bid goodbye to her, feeling quite like a Shakespearean character out of one of his several tragic stories.

Perhaps, she could sense my feelings again, as she gave me a tight hug and whispered, "I hope we meet the coming weekend."

I held her slightly longer than the courtesies demand in such situations and walked away with a hope that such a gesture would trigger some feelings in her. As the distance between our physical bodies increased, my desire to run back and hold her in my arms increased proportionately. I walked like a zombie till I got seated.

'What is happening to me?' I thought as the forewarning of the astrologer, a few years back echoed in my mind – *You are going to fall in love during the period of Venus in Rahu. Chances of this happening overseas are higher because of the placement of Venus in your twelfth house.* Scientific or not, for the first time, I liked astrology. With my spirits undergoing a sinusoidal curve fluctuation, I decided to flatten the graphs by requesting the air hostess to fetch me a double Glenfiddich on the rocks. I put on my favourite music, pulled back my seat, and thought about her curls flirting with her cheeks and the rhythmic motions of her hands as she talked. With a blissful smile on my face and a glass of spirit in my hand, I didn't know when I went off to sleep.

For the next couple of days, I was busy in setting up my booth in the "Expo Guadalajara". I had hired Maria as my interpreter and as an assistant during the exhibition. She was a young college-going girl who had taken a week off to make some quick money and also to gain some experience. She was so efficient in handling secretarial work that I thought of offering her a permanent job in our office in India.

We finished making up the stall by early noon on the second day. As we had nothing else to do, Maria offered to show me around the beautiful city of Guadalajara. We spent a good amount of time viewing the Instituto Cultural Cabanas.

"The Cabanas is a UNESCO World Heritage site and is famous for series of murals made by Orozco in the 1930s," explained Maria.

We had an excellent lunch at La Chata which was serving authentic Mexican food, quite appealing to the Indian palate. It was during the main course that she mentioned, "If you have time, we could go to the city of Tequila after the exhibition as it is just an hour's drive from here."

Not that I had not thought about Manvi since I had last met her, but it was then that the floodgates of memories opened and I got lost in Manvi's thoughts. Maria dropped me back to my hotel Crowne Plaza as I continued to stay deluged with the persona of Manvi.

We got busy for the next few days in the exhibition. It was real hard work answering questions to various enquiries. But since potential customers and new orders were being generated, my spirits were up. We even had a visit from the Indian embassy people to buck us up.

The beauty quotient in the exhibition was pretty high. The booth from Far East Asia in front of us had unusual crowd because they had the two prettiest local hostesses in the show. The best part was that during the non-peak hours they would often come to our booth to chat with us. I guess Indian and Mexican people have some karmic connection. We eat similar food, we are similar looking in general terms, and we are kind of growing economies. I was amazed that they knew about our film industry, our yoga techniques, and about Taj Mahal. It was a pity though that I had to use Maria's linguistic skills to communicate with them.

During our free time, we wrote emails back to office and to the visitors. On the last day Maria asked me again if I had any plans to visit nearby areas as the weekend was on. I politely declined her as I had made up my mind not to go to Tequila village. We packed our samples and posters on the last afternoon and came back to the hotel where I paid off Maria and bid her goodbye. She had come really close to me as a co-worker in the last few days, and it was a sad moment to see her off.

I went back to my room and packed my luggage. I then went to the bar to have a couple of drinks. The bar menu was full of various Tequila drinks. I was recommended Bandera, named after the colours of the flag of Mexico. It had three shot glasses filled with green lime juice, white Tequila, and red Sangrita. The barman advised me to sip or drink straight, depending upon my capacity. Although my drinking capacities are inclined towards the former, the manliness in me erred me into drinking straight. The barman gave me an approving look as I nodded for a repeat.

We got chatting and I bought a drink for him. He coaxed me that I needed to visit the village of Tequila. He then proceeded to give me complete knowledge of various Tequila drinks and their manufacturing process.

Sitting in the bar, I reached a point where I could see only Manvi in all the bottles. Even the shape of some bottles resembled the slender physique of Manvi. The talk of Tequila and the magic of Manvi had made me decide that I would visit Tequila village the next morning. I thanked the barman, tipped him, and left for a quick bite. Manvi was with me all the time till I came back to my room and slept.

I woke up early the next morning with a sprightly feeling, in anticipation of meeting Manvi, though I had a heavy head due to my last night's excesses. I felt much better after the shower and after having spent considerable time on the top deck. I was a serious believer that looks are temporary and class is permanent, but perhaps that spring in my step, after having received due inputs from the heart, as any Shakespearean would agree or from the mind, as any scientific person would have vouched for, although my inclination on that particular morning would have been heavily tilted towards the former, made me hum my favourite song.

The morning was beautiful, the buffet breakfast was excellent, and the people around me looked full of life, mainly attributed to the most desired anticipation of seeing her once again. All seemed well with God and His world. The portrait of life was so variedly hued today.

The concierge booked a ticket of a tourist coach for me that was coming to the hotel for a pickup at nine in the morning.

Tequila is located about 60 km away from Guadalajara on the way to Puerto Vallarta. It is best known as being the birthplace of the drink that bears its name, 'Tequila', which is made from the blue agave plant, native to this area. Our coach driver, Angeles, turned out to be a very interesting commentator as well. He continued to give us a detailed briefing about the history and distilleries of Tequila village which today is a World Heritage Site. After about three-quarters-of-an-hour drive, he pulled up the coach amidst a big field of agave plants.

As we got off, we were introduced to Jimador, the man who harvests agave plants. He was an imposing man wearing a faded blue jeans, white shirt with two buttons open, a wide Mexican hat, big leather boots and a belt, holding a semicircular blade at the end of a long pole in his hand. Almost everybody on board took turns to get their pictures clicked with him.

The distillery guide then led us through the entire Tequila-making process till bottling. The distillery had a nice tasting table set up so that everyone could taste four different kinds of drinks on the house.

As I sipped my drink, my thoughts returned to my last meeting with Manvi. With Samar around, I wasn't sure of the reception I would get. The thought of Manvi had my pulse racing but I got stuck with a roadblock. The thought of Samar and the words of *Panditji* came haunting back to me – *You will never get the girl of your dreams.* We got back on the road and my journey continued through rolling hills and dwindling thoughts.

"This is Tequila," announced Angeles as we drove past a cluster of locals wearing cowboy boots and hats. The coach dropped us at the Parish church near the centre of the town and announced that we had six hours with us to paint the town red. It was there that I heard my phone ring.

"*Hola,* Ashwin! *Como estas.*" Her melodious voice, so full of energy, came through.

I very much wanted to say *te amo* but settled for a more friendly and sophisticated *hola.*

"Where are you?" she quizzed.

"In Tequila near the church," I said.

"Oh, that's great. We are at the Black Crow. This is located in the centre of the village. It will not take you more than a few minutes to reach us. See you soon," she said and dropped the call.

The word *we* made me nervous again. The 'very self-confident and suave' me, the 'well-qualified and highly travelled' me, the 'outgoing and marketing expert' me was a fit case of nerves for my neurosurgeon friend back in Ludhiana.

I slowly strolled towards one of the largest distilleries by the name of Jose Cuervo. The word *Cuervo* is Spanish for crow and sure enough, the entrance was highlighted by a giant sculpture of a black crow. On the face of it I was looking at the black crow, whereas, inwardly my thoughts were with my poor sparrow in the clutches of the *we* vulture.

As I neared the rendezvous point, I made an effort to become conscious of my surroundings. The complex was built on typical colonial pattern of construction. Several courtyards with colourful gift shops and sitting areas were hosting the visitors. Just across the street was a museum which apparently had all sorts of original equipment related to Tequila-making process on display.

I spotted the two of them just next to the entrance. Perhaps my reflexes had been dimmed by the generous helping of Tequila or by the *we* pressure, I didn't know which factor outweighed the other, but what I knew was the presence of Manvi had floored my already depleted nerves.

May be Samar had sensed my anxiety or perhaps, he had the first-mover advantage in free wine tasting. It was the one-upmanship trait of his personality, when he said, "Hope you had plenty of free samples to last through the day." He burst out laughing while shaking my hand.

Comfortingly, Manvi sprang to my defence and said, "Cut it out, Samar . . ."

She gave me a big hug as she said, "I knew you would come, Ashwin."

Samar then guided us to the courtyard where we sat down in the open under a shady tree. The courtyard was full of people in their colourful dresses, trying various drinks along with mouth-watering Mexican snacks – nachos with salsa and sour cream, duros, baked tortilla chips, taco dips, and many more.

Manvi wanted to start with Margarita, a cocktail consisting of Tequila mixed with orange flavoured liqueur and lime juice served with salt on the glass rim. This gave me a chance to flaunt my recently acquired knowledge about the local drink to good use. I thanked my barman friend of the last night as I ordered the next drink, lick-sip-suck shots. Now I am not a very jealous person by nature, but the occasion demanded the vice, so I began my monologue.

I said, "These single shots are often served with salt and slice of lime. The drinker moistens the back of the hand and pours on the salt. The salt is licked, the Tequila is drunk, and fruit slice is quickly bitten. Salt lessens the burn of Tequila and sour fruit balances and enhances the flavour. We had actually tried out a variation of these shots during our college days at the Nutties Club party. We used to put the shots, salt, and fruit in a *golgappa* and eat them in one go. So these were baptised as *golgappa shots*."

Having won the first round of war, I pulled back a little to consolidate, as any guerrilla-warfare strategist would do to check the amount of damage done and to bask in its momentary glory. But unfortunately, not much damage had been done. I thought of changing my strategy and decided to downgrade my aggression.

"Be in control and think like David," I told my mind. My competitor was indeed a Goliath in terms of overall superiority. A picture-perfect Samar had an excellent way with ladies and according to the feedback I had, he was a very noble person. In comparison, I was a little better than average-looking and had just enough money for a good life. Plainly from Manvi's perspective, the chasm between the two of us was significant.

"There must be some chinks in his armour," I thought as I decided to be patient.

We decided to do some general *dekkho* of the village town. Manvi excitingly suggested that she had seen some gypsies camping on the other side of the town and she wanted to visit them. Since the suggestion had come from her, Samar immediately jumped to his feet. I being in dovish mode, looked into the sparrow's eyes and waited till she kind of coaxed me to walk the walk. I do not know which law of physics applies to this eye-contact thing with one's heart-throb which gives much more yield than any of the known lever does.

In my younger days, I had studied for two years in Udaipur, better known as the City of Lakes in the royal Indian state of Rajasthan. I had a chance to interact with the Indian gypsies, known as *banjaras*, when we had gone on a Scouts' trip to Bikaner, another beautiful and ethnic town of Rajasthan.

Their womenfolk often wear very colourful and beautiful costumes called *ghagra cholis* which are decorated with mirrors, chips and coins, and glittery sequins. They adorn their rugged hands with dark henna and their arms with tattoos and thick ivory bangles. Both men and women wear big silver amulets in ankles, large nose rings, and have their hair pleated. My impression was that they were always singing and dancing in spite of their hardships. They were travelling craftsmen by day and entertainers by night.

Those images came rushing back to me as we walked into the colourful gypsy camp. Goats and cows were grazing around, the black rooster with the bright red hackle was perched on a fencepost and was constantly crowing, the donkeys were resting by the side of carts, and a few men could be seen working with metals. About a dozen kids, vibrantly dressed, could be seen playing *atrapadas*, the *catch-catch* game, without being hung up for being deficient in permanence of their existence.

Manvi was thrilled to be there as the journalist in her came to foray. She took a number of pictures and tried to speak to the children who shied away.

"Do you know gypsies have extraordinary fortune-telling abilities and they have remarkable psychic abilities," Manvi informed us.

I did not want to say 'no' to Manvi but my disbelief did not let me say 'yes'. So I chose to be quiet while Samar walked towards the kids, took out some chocolates from his pocket and distributed among them. The kids were hovering around him as he started talking to them animatedly.

Very soon, he called aloud, "They say that the third tent on the right, that yellow-coloured one, there's an old lady who is extremely good with the crystal ball predictions."

Samar ran back, held Manvi's hand, and rushed towards the yellow tent with me in a distant tow.

At the entry, like a true gentleman, Samar got into a position to knock at the door but seeing the futility of his action, he coughed lightly, lifted the flap, and walked into the tent pulling Manvi along.

I was a few steps behind. I was in a dilemma whether to walk in or not. Had Manvi waited for me or had she called for me, I would have been glad to be by her side, but since neither happened, I found myself left out and became melancholic. I felt as if my favourite toy had been snatched away from me. I was weak-kneed, with a lump in my throat.

I died a thousand deaths waiting for Manvi to come out. After all Samar was good-looking, rich, lively, and an accomplished man. Too suitable!

"Why wouldn't Manvi choose him over me," I thought. *Panditji's* prophecy, *You will never get the girl you like*, haunted me once again.

"Ch . . . ch." I heard this sound from nowhere. I looked up and visualised the now familiar Rahu, the boxer-in–blue, sitting atop the adjacent red tent, signifying a complete victory. I dropped my head in self-pity. I did not have the heart to reply back. There was hardly any heart left.

"Hello, sir." A male voice shook me out of my gloom.

I turned towards the direction of the sound. But the vision was hazy as two droplets descended from my eyes. In a hurry to keep the secret of my grief, my hand rushed towards my face.

"Hello," I reciprocated, though mindlessly.

"Is everything all right, sir?" the boy asked me.

I gave him a long look. He wore a custom-tailored gypsy outfit with a red-and-white-dotted bandana, white puffed full-sleeves shirt, and high-waist black trousers. A broad belt separated the tucked-in shirt and the trousers. The earrings completed the accessorised look.

"Do you need anything, sir?" His hospitality was well loaded with concern.

I gathered myself and told him that I was fine but I expressed my utter astonishment on how he was speaking such fluent English.

"Sir, our ancestors were from Romania. I stayed with my granny in England for a few years," he clarified.

"Oh! I see," I replied.

"You too have come to see Grandma?" he asked.

The intensity of surprise was much more this time as I was clueless who was he talking about.

"The crystal ball reader," he said, pointing towards the yellow tent. "Everybody who comes here loves to see her," he took pride in saying so.

"Oh! Is she your grandma?" I didn't wait for an answer and continued, "No, I am not interested as I don't believe in impossibilities."

He got settled on a tree stub behind him, smiled and spoke philosophically, "She is not just a crystal ball reader or a soothsayer. She has been blessed with extrasensory powers since she was a child."

I realised that I was being insensitive. Just to make him feel better, I said, "Oh great! The tourists must be thronging her."

"Yes, sir." He nodded and continued, "She is generally very pleasant and courteous with everybody, but if she likes somebody, she comes into her element, and what philosophy and poetry flows as she predicts! Truly wondrous."

I asked, "Poetic? Philosophical?" I didn't want to be rude but to possess such elite virtues wasn't expected out of gypsies. The surprise in my voice was quite evident.

"Yes, she is . . . " He couldn't speak further as a giggle distracted us.

It was Manvi. Both of them had emerged from the tent, smiling and more importantly, Samar was holding her hand.

On seeing me, her expression changed into a question. "Why didn't you come in, Ashwin?" Looking at Samar she continued, "She is so good. No, Samar?"

Samar nodded and addressed me, "Yes! Rush in, man. She has already been paid for you also."

I ignored him, but the hurt was too grave to be ignored. If affluence was his virtue, its use was vicious.

"I wanted to give you privacy to discuss your personal questions," I replied.

Perhaps Samar's talk about money had hurt me further or perhaps I was sulking because it wasn't me. Never in my life had anybody else's money bothered me, then why that day, I thought.

"Privacy?" she repeated. The way she spoke this word, it was quite clear that she couldn't comprehend my justification.

"Let us go. I don't want to see her," I told them firmly.

All my resistance vanished with the mere touch of her hand as she caught hold of my hand and led me towards the entrance. I hoped that she would follow me in, but that did not happen. I could hear their animated voices fading away as she pushed me inside and left.

The darkness inside was in complete contrast to the outer vibrancy. A dim bulb hanging from the centre of the roof was the only source of light. A conical aluminium shade surrounding the bulb tried but failed to focus the pale light on to the crystal ball placed on a table covered with a black cloth.

Everything was so still inside that I could hear my own heartbeat. I was still struggling to find my moorings when I got startled to see a pair of dark red eyes, like balls of fire, staring at me from the darkness in the far right corner of the tent.

I stood still for a while deliberating my next move. "What am I doing out here?" I questioned myself.

I was caught unaware the second time around as I heard a deep commanding voice, "Come here and sit down."

It was the old gypsy lady calling me. For a gypsy, she spoke wonderful English.

My feet dragged me in the direction of the sound.

The chair made a squeaky noise as I sat down. My eyes were still fixed in the far-right corner.

"Do not be afraid. That is Siju, my pet rabbit," she spoke very affectionately, trying to calm me down.

I let out a sigh of relief and directed my attention to the lady. My eyes had got used to the darkness by then. Even in the dim light, the wrinkles caused by years of nomadic wandering, were visible on her face and hands. She had grey hair, blue eyes, and a big forehead. She was wearing a black scarf covering half her head.

She looked at me for a short while and then focused her gaze on the crystal ball. After a couple of moments, she cried out loud, "Oh God! This is so scary!"

I felt a chill going down my spine as I heard this. I was in no mood to handle any more eerie forebodings. I got up to go.

She waved towards me to stop as she kept on looking at the crystal ball. Slowly her expression changed. She looked calmer.

Her motherly voice sounded again, "Come here, son. Do not be afraid."

I obeyed like a child.

She made me sit in a chair by her side. She held my hand, gazed into the crystal, and spoke softly, "Look here. That is you, my son. You are in trouble now."

I tried to peep into the crystal ball but could hardly see anything.

She continued her monologue, "You are a destiny's child, my son. But a dreaded enemy blocks your way. If you can decipher what I prophesize, you will achieve what you want to."

She pulled out a piece of paper and a pen from below the table and asked me to write what she spoke.

The thrill on her face was visible as she uttered, "Yes! . . . after so many days . . . Oh! It's really intriguing, so interesting. I am now going to make some life-changing prophecies for you."

She went on and on without realising what I was going through.

"Write down," she commanded.

I started scribbling reluctantly as she spoke.

Perched high, light in the sky vast; looketh for solace, in the past;

Eastern art from ancient time; renders me the key, that maketh self prime.

After jotting down the first couplet, I realised that it was more of a riddle, which hardly made any sense to me.

My reluctance changed into an eerie feeling as she spelt out the next one.

Apparition blueth on the back, like a boulder;
Changeth white, on his shoulder.

'Apparition blueth'!!! These two words thronged me with the creepy description of the blue dragon by *Pandit* Sharma in Chandigarh. I shivered. My blood ran cold as the words of the old gypsy lady fell on my ears. Was it a coincidence? It was so uncanny! My mind went numb and my hand-mind coordination went haywire. I stopped writing.

Was it her extrasensory power? How could she enter my mind and read what had been happening to me? This was unbelievable and so unreal. I wondered, "How the astrologer Anand Sharma and the clairvoyant gypsy lady arrived at the same conclusion – *apparition blueth on the back*. There had to be a method to this madness!"

The old lady looked at me, smiled, and said mysteriously, "Please write down, son. Someday you will thank me for this."

I somehow managed to scribble the remaining riddles. She kept on talking to me for a few more minutes. There was a mystic glow on her face as she spoke for one last time, "Remember, these are not riddles but gems given to you today, son. Understand them, and fight your fight. You shall win. There is no pain time cannot dilute . . . Seek and actualise the reasons of your existence, coded in these four riddles."

Although I did not completely understand what she meant but her final words surely induced an incredible faith in me. I had always been a staunch believer in the *karma* theory and that day's experience indicated some enterprise on my part, that was bound to influence the times to come. It surely left me with a good feeling.

There was a big grin on my face as I bid her goodbye and walked out. Finally, Ashwin the winner was back. The destiny child was back.

Manvi and Samar waved at me from a distance. I waved back. They were enjoying some kind of a gypsy ice lolly.

I looked atop the red tent on my right but saw nothing.

I couldn't discern that a chance visit to a gypsy would change my life so much. The mystery of the riddles prophesized by the mystic wanderer had to be unravelled!

"Ice cream?" Manvi asked as she slurped on one.

"No, thanks," I replied.

We walked back to the centre of the town. We bought some souvenirs, and soon it was time for us to leave. Manvi had to head for Mazatlan, Samar stayed in a local hotel, and I came back to Guadalajara.

I had a late-night American Airlines flight to Miami connecting to Delhi. It was during the flight to Delhi that I took out the gypsy's paper and read out the second riddle again.

"How did the old gypsy know about the *blue apparition*? How did she know about *Rahu*?" I asked myself as I struggled for an answer.

Just then a smartly dressed air hostess served hot coffee. As I relished my cup of coffee, I was transported nine years back to that eventful evening in Chandigarh, when I had a meeting with the astrologer, *Pandit* Anand Sharma. I still remember the conversation I had with my friend Abir in our favourite coffee shop, later that evening. That was the day when *apparition blueth on the back* had metaphored.

That was the day *Rahu was born*.

The period of Rahu has started which is going to control your life for the next eighteen years . . . a period of struggle, frustration, failure, and heartbreaks . . . Rahu is the mighty and naughty child of Maya and will create illusions and make you manipulative . . .

Astro speaks

Chapter 2

Rahu Is Born . . .

Sitting in the Delhi bound flight, I vividly remembered that evening nine years back.

It was darker than usual, the sky was cast with French loaves, a loose bunch of stubborn and unmanageable dark grey cotton candies, lined with orange tinge. The sweet and young pre-monsoon showers were flirting with the dusky moist and fragrant outer aura of the city beautiful, Chandigarh, partially obscuring the picturesque Shivalik ranges in the background.

I walked by the eroded valley of a seasonal rivulet which had been retained by the town planners and sculptured into a continuum of evergreen foliage.

Clouded by inner dilemmas, I could hardly enjoy the beauty as I reluctantly walked towards the office of the astrologer, *Pandit* Anand Sharma.

The mere view of the extended tarpaulin shed of the teashop under the huge *peepal* tree, as mentioned in the address written on the crumpled parchment, made me realise that I had almost reached my destination. I looked up at the sky which was not too fair, though the time was just around 4.45 p.m. A soft droplet on my left eyelid soaked my lashes and forced me to close my eyes for a wee bit.

29

"*Chai*?" the shrilly question of the tea shop owner hardly gave me time to rub off the itchy wetness.

For a fraction of a second, I looked at the enticing steaming pan on the earthen oven in which the tea was coming to a boil.

"*Pandit* Anand Sharma . . . ?" I asked, the question more in my eyes than on my lips.

"Go upstairs." He pointed at a narrow one-foot-wide staircase across the road, while dexterously juggling the stream of tea into chipped glasses from an unreasonable height.

I looked at that mysterious tunnel and very unlike me, I couldn't help perceiving it as a pathway to the end of my woes. A smile appeared on my face. The staircase to the astrologer's charismatic and mystic den had probably never experienced such an inquisitive yet withdrawn climber as me. My thoughtful climb was interrupted as I raised my eyes. A shadowy figure seemed to overpower me and a shrill tone pierced through my eardrums. "*Bhaiya!* Wait . . . let me go down first." After a brief brushing struggle with that plump lady, I finally managed to reach the top.

I stepped into an unkempt lobby which served as a waiting room for *Panditji's* customers. I looked around the purple-painted room, soaked in the musty aroma of heavily perfumed incense sticks. I noticed four people sitting in the lobby, but my eyes came to rest on the receptionist sitting in the left corner, with a worn-out register in front of her. Her eyes were continuously glued to the small TV running a Hindi movie, with the sound tuned down. Her disinterest in my arrival conveyed that I had apparently disturbed her movie-watching ritual. Still looking at the screen, she hurriedly demanded, "Fifty rupees ".

I gingerly took out the money from my pocket and handed it over to her.

Looking at the red-faced clay statue of a monkey placed on a shelf, a little above her head, I said, "I am Ashwin. I have the appointment at five o'clock."

She impatiently took the money and waved towards a sofa with worn-out, probably maroon in colour, tapestry. I looked at the dust-covered rotary-type black phone on her table and moved disgustingly towards the sofa. As I sat down I could feel the squeaky springs hitting me back. I changed my stance a little so as to cause uniform distribution of my body's load on the sofa. I noticed a pile of newspapers and magazines, sans covers, on a small table a few feet away. I was tempted to reach out for them, but the effort to recreate a balanced sit-down posture kept me from getting up. My eyes glanced at another door which probably led to *Panditji's* office.

"*Jyotish Acharya*," I murmured to myself as I read *Panditji's* certificate hanging on the wall, right next to his picture in which he was receiving award from some local organisation.

"At least they could try to keep the place clean," I thought as my eyes settled on an inverter by my side, with permanent marks of dirt on it.

I cursed my encounter of that morning with my friend Kabir, who was an ardent fan of *Panditji*. My circumstances had, perhaps, momentarily weakened me and I had agreed. Otherwise me? Visiting an astrologer!

Actually, I had an early-morning altercation with my boss. Probably, it was telling on my face as I was sitting in the office cafeteria.

"Why so sad and sullen, Ashwin?" quizzed Kabir as he pulled a chair next to mine.

I had no answer but my long face said it all.

"Your stars seem to be playing games which you need to understand, Ashwin," he said while relishing his burger.

"Bullshit . . ." I remarked.

But my logical ridicule didn't seem to dishearten him because he continued, "I am telling you, Ashwin, why do you think that such a bright, enterprising man isn't the blue-eyed baby of the boss? Nothing good is happening to you. Why? You have been having mishaps one after the other in the recent past. Why?"

"Well, I am a man of scientific temperament. I am an engineer. How can I? I mean, I don't believe in all this nonsense," I protested vehemently.

"You have nothing to lose if you visit him once," pleaded Kabir.

This was the final clincher as he proceeded authoritatively to set up a meeting that very evening. He made a road map and thrust it in my pocket as he walked out and said, "I would have come with you but the boss has asked me to rush to Baddi to get the frames' design, and Panditji is off to Delhi tomorrow. So you have to go alone today only. 5 p.m. sharp. Okay?"

And so here I was, trying to get my problems solved by someone who could, laughably, change my future. I thought so giving a cursory glance to my surroundings.

"Anil Sharma," the receptionist called out aloud as the door to *Panditji's* cabin opened and a young couple walked out, lost in their discussion. Anil, sitting on the sofa next to me, sprang to his feet and walked towards the cabin, leaving me with the tough task of readjusting and realigning the balance of recoiling spring forces on my rear. He removed his shoes before walking into the main office. I could sense that he was very nervous.

"Excuse me!" I heard someone addressing me. As I turned my head around, I saw her for the first time.

She had a beautiful doe-eyed face, too charming for the eyes to be taken off her. Her gesture to shrink her physical being indicated that my gaze embarrassed her. Perhaps, she could feel the touch of my eyes on her face. A strange feeling took over me as if I had known her for a long, long time.

"Do you mind if we go in before you?" she requested. Her voice was soft, gentle, courteous, and low.

I nodded my head as if in a trance and said, "Please do."

I liked the locks of her hair falling on her face. She was wearing a white *salwar kameez* and was continuously adjusting her *dupatta*. She was accompanied by an elderly woman, most likely her mother.

I liked Kabir at that moment.

A few minutes later, Anil walked out of *Panditji's* room with a relieved face. His nervousness seemed to have vanished. This ticked a positive in my mind in favour of the *problem-solver*.

I turned my head and watched the girl take off her white sandals, rather clumsily, outside the door. I wanted to get up and give her a hand to prevent her from falling as she hopped on one foot, with the silver anklet getting disturbed. Her facial expressions changed with every action of hers. As she passed through the door, her *dupatta* got stuck and I could see her frowning.

"Beautiful." The word was so apt for her as she turned back to get her robe unstuck. She was mumbling to herself as she pulled hard. Her eyes shut momentarily, and she finally managed the operation successfully.

Now the room had just me and the receptionist who was continually watching her lifeline. I was comparatively in a happier state of mind as I waited for my turn. After about twenty-five minutes of waiting, the girl walked out. She was not looking very happy and the elderly lady, who followed her, looked circumspect.

I tried to make an eye contact, but she was lost in some other world as she passed by with an unintentional indifference. I wanted to know her name, instead the dreary sound of the receptionist knocked me back into the real world. "Ashwin," she called out aloud.

A fear of the unknown gripped me as my own problems came haunting back. I took off my shoes, following my predecessors, and entered the ten-by-ten cabin.

I had not known at that time that in the next fifteen minutes my life would turn upside down.

The cabin was dimly lit. It had a table with two visitor chairs and a big black imposing office chair of *Panditji*. There was an old computer on the table, a printer on one side, and several yellow-coloured horoscopes lying in a pile on the other side. Pictures of several deities were adorning the walls. On the left side of the room was a cupboard with glass panes, containing brass plates embossed with all kinds of geometrical patterns.

I greeted the rotund looking *Panditji* with a *namaste,* and he asked me to sit down. He was dressed up in a white *kurta pajama*, had a big red *tikka* on his forehead and interestingly, his every finger had a ring with a different-coloured stone. He had a red-and-yellow *mauli*, the holy thread, tied to his right wrist and had a *rudraksh mala* around his neck.

He asked me about the date, time, and place of my birth and proceeded to type it on a rickety keyboard, with most of the letters and figures faded. He then drew my horoscope on a piece of paper giving numbers and star positions to different boxes. He pulled out a log book from his drawer and added some more information to the chart. His grave expressions were further enhanced as he twisted his lips exposing his lower teeth, which probably, had never been scaled.

"Your period of *Rahu* has started which is going to control your life for the next eighteen years," he said grimly.

"So . . ." was all that came out of my mouth as my heart pounded. As a layman, I could only comprehend that I was in for some misfortune.

"This is a period where *Rahu*, your *maha dasa* planet, is not favourably placed. This is a period of struggle, heartbreaks, failures, and downfalls", he prophesied.

I was dumbstruck!

I mean, my life had just begun. Eighteen years is a long time. The prime span of the short-lived human life of a vivacious, suave, and idyllic young man was pronounced to be going into halves. *Panditji's* forecast very explicitly predicted that an era was going to be ushered into my life which might not be cherished with any fancies in the times to come and the hitherto-unknown-to-me *Rahu* would be responsible to chariotest laughs and twinkles out of my life.

I gathered my wits to counter his projections and spoke, rather defensively, "Barring the last few months, I have had a wonderful life. I was always a meritorious student. I was among the top ten rankers in the state entrance test. I held many responsible and coveted posts in my college and had graduated in the top five of my batch. I was probably the best all-round student during my MBA at Panjab University."

"That was in the period of Mars, my boy. Now your *Rahu* has started." *Panditji* raised his chin and brows at the same time and spoke with a dash of sarcasm, "It will make you take wrong decisions, and you will run after illusions. You will travel a lot, but the struggle to achieve your goals will go on. Success will come in patches and that too after a lot of effort."

He went on as an anchor of a horrifying documentary on my future, "Your best-laid plans will go up in smoke. You will never get the girl you dream of. However, the aspect of *Rahu* on your ascendant will make you the master of manipulation which will help you in partial achievement of your goals."

I was shocked to hear this. I muttered, "Manipulative . . . me . . . ?"

Panditji replied with a wily smile on his face, "Yes, manipulative! The placement of *Rahu Maharaj* in your *kundali* is such that you will become very scheming and calculative."

I was getting deflated by the moment. Nervously shifting my bulk in the chair, I asked again, "What . . . What is this *Rahu*?"

Panditji rocked back in his chair, looked into my eyes, his smile getting wilier as he said, "*Rahu* is the dragon head of an *asura* that swallows the sun, causing eclipses . . ."

"I thought eclipses are caused when . . ." I interrupted but was cut short by *Panditji* as he raised his hand to stop me. He was in the driver's seat and wanted no unscheduled stoppage.

Having achieved his objective of silencing me, he slowly lowered his hand and continued, pointing his finger towards his left, without turning his head as his eyes continued to stare at me, "Look at that picture on your right."

Quickly following the command, I glanced at my right and returned my gaze back to *Panditji,* not quite understanding what he wanted to convey.

"That is *Shri Rahu ji*!" he exclaimed and carried on, "*Shri Rahu* is a malefic shadow planet which has a distinct, profound, and predictable impact on human lives. He is a legendary master of deception and is a significator of cheaters, insincere people, and immoral acts."

"If he is deceptive, then why do you address him so respectfully?" I argued.

Panditji laughed scornfully at my half-baked knowledge and said, "*Rahu* is supposed to be a mighty and naughty child of *Maya*, and thus has lot of dualities attached to its illusory nature."

"Dualities?" I interrupted again in a slur, as my mouth had gone dry.

"Yes. *Rahu* is negatively placed in your horoscope. Therefore, its period of eighteen years will that be of agony and chaos in your life. Most importantly, *Rahu's* influence is more on the mental level than on the physical one as during this period your mind will get misled and mental tension will increase," he replied.

He then visually scanned my birth chart, placed his pen on the tenth house, and said, "Had your *Rahu* been here it would have given you big name, fame, and luck. *Shri Rahu* is also the significator of electric lights and is also known as the artificial night sun. Do you understand now?"

He gave me a long look and went back to study my chart. There was a censored silence in the room. The lull gave me time to recoup as I started looking around the pictures of deities on the walls. I wanted to make an eye contact with them, but their visions too seemed to be as hazy as mine. The reasons were different though. Perhaps they could not see beyond their eyes, smudged with *tikkas* put on them religiously by *Panditji,* and my vision was afflicted by *Rahu* already.

My mouth went from dry to parched as my eyes rested on the picture of *Rahu* to my right. As I made an effort to zoom into the surprisingly still not smeared eyes of my unwanted foe for the next eighteen years, I felt a dreary chill go down my spine. *Rahu's* sinister eyes had come alive, as if they were blazing with a sort of demonic fury, watching me with sadistic pleasure. The picture of *Rahu* appeared spooky and had a smoky appearance with a blue physique. The face was broad, the jaws were large in the shape of a square, and the nose was big and flat. Two dracula teeth on the sides were protruding out like fangs from the blood-red lips. The giant ears were largely obscured by black curly locks. The bushy handlebar moustache, thick and dense, was frightfully curled up, ironically towards the heavens. The top of the head was covered by a colourful yet ghastly looking headgear with horns, images of dog heads, and serpents.

A resounding "Yes" from *Panditji* suddenly brought my imagery to a halt, and my hope-studded eyelids looked disbelievingly at him.

"Do not worry. *Upaay hai iska*. I will write down some remedies, and you follow these to minimise the effect of *Rahu*. I will also make a ring for you which will help you tremendously," he spoke with great conviction.

I did not know what to do next. I genuinely felt the absence of Kabir at that time.

"For immediate relief, I can perform *puja* for you," *Panditji* suggested further, trying to size me up.

"How much?" I coughed lightly and asked.

"Eleven thousand rupees for *puja*. The Gomedh stone will be for Rs. 5,100. You have to wear it in silver in your middle finger on Saturday," *Panditji* pitched rather politely.

"Capitalising on my woes," I thought but said nothing.

Seeing my reluctance to reply, he wrote some *upaayas* on his notepad and handed it over to me and said in a politically sweet vein, "You can come back whenever you want your *puja* to be performed."

I thanked him and got up from my chair. I took one final look at the picture on my right. I felt as if *Rahu* in the picture had come alive and jumped on to my shoulders. I turned around and walked, with a heavy weight pinning me down, out into the lobby where there were two more sacrificial lambs now awaiting their turns. The receptionist, least sensitive to the plight of the victims of fate or may be of her boss, was still glued to the TV as I moved out of the lobby.

Walking down the stairs, I had an eerie feeling of the blue mass of *Rahu* weighing me down which reminded me of a childhood story in which King Vikram carried a phantom on his shoulders.

The air was quite still outside as a promenade of lights was coming to life. As the astrological jargons made their way into my conscious and subconscious mind, I hastened my pace through the moist, dusky road laden with trees on both sides, trying to leave the hellish abode of pedantry as far and as soon as possible.

It had started drizzling as I reached Willow café, my favourite coffee shop. I walked in and settled on a sofa chair in my preferred corner. In no time, Jack served me a hot, frothy cappuccino with the familiar smile of his. Jack knew my taste by now. I eased into the sofa further as the echo of *Panditji's* words continued to haunt me deep down. "Struggling, failed, frustrated, manipulative, scheming, . . . me?"

The *Rahu* was born. The destiny child lay in tatters.

"Excuse me, sir," the voice of the air hostess brought me out of my recall.

I handed her over the empty cup of coffee and requested for a refill.

I was forced to think that my visit to Panditji years back and the prophecy of the gypsy, 'apparition blueth on the back, like a boulder' were reflecting ominous similarities which had my pulse racing.

I sipped my coffee miles above the ocean and remembered how I had fought back on that fateful evening in the Willow café, how I had sought inspiration from my past.

The destiny child in me had retaliated loudly, "Manipulative . . . me? Shouldn't be me! Can't be me!"

Be tough, yet be compassionate . . . Be a leader . . . Do great things that the world remembers you for . . . You are destined to do great things, my boy . . .

My father

Chapter 3

The Destiny Child

I had been born a destiny child, or so my father thought. I still remember that day very distinctly.

We lived in a palatial cantonment bungalow, reminiscent of the days of British regime. Bejewelled by a luxuriant green lawn, fringed with rich green shrubbery, it could simply take your breath away. More so, on a moist monsoon evening, when standing at the far end of the lawn, the ancient banyan tree's hanging roots looked darker and mysterious to my young eyes. Moss-green hanging flora, in the never-ending, pillared verandah, was no less than the wet lace teasing the bare and fair dewy arms of a maiden. Duskier than usual, the evening made way for the lamps to glow, well before time. The crossed metallic full length spears at the entrance, dispelling sheen in the soft glow of the lamps, so suitably defined the taste of the denizens.

I still remember the aroma of chicken curry which took all the skills of Mom, despite the help of the cook.

Sitting on a sofa, I was fully engrossed in my favourite Hardy Boys. A rustle of the white net curtain made me look that side. That was Dad with a drink in his hand and a smile on his face. He looked at me lovingly.

"That's like my son," he said, patting my shoulder. He was always very expressive about his love.

It thundered outside.

"Look at this boy. Still not back home. He and his football," he grumbled his concern for my elder brother, who had been out with his friends since early evening.

He stood next to the fireplace, lost in his reverie.

He spoke after a while, "Ashwin, put on the gramophone. Let's hear Johnny Cash."

I put on the LP record of his liking.

"Come here, I'll tell you something," he called me.

As I walked up to him, he put his hand on my shoulder and looked at the life-size portrait of my grandfather, hanging above the fireplace, in our gigantic, high-roof room.

He could still stand smartly even after downing Old Monk fivers. "That is the Indian Order of Merit medallion around his neck," my father said proudly.

"My boy, IOM was the second highest gallantry decoration that a native member of the British Indian Army could receive," the Colonel reminisced, looking at the historic Captain's picture and continued, imbibing in me a solid value system. "Be tough yet compassionate. Be a leader. Do great things that the world remembers you for. You are destined to do great things, my boy."

I simply nodded, not quite understanding his own unfulfilled desires, caused by partition-affected relocation.

My father being an army man, I had a great childhood growing up in pristine and evergreen cantonments. My passion for reading grew in that vibrant environment as we graduated from Tintins to Enid Blytons to Ayn Rands. I topped the board exams in the district and went on to become the captain of my school, the following year.

"He will top the entrance exam for National Defence Academy," my father would often tell my mom. It was therefore, nothing short of catastrophe that I was categorised in the Medical Board, due to a flatfoot, after having done exceedingly well during the exams and SSB interview.

Engineering was the next best option and a top ten ranking in the entrance test brought me to the city which was to shape my destiny. I joined the prestigious Mechanical department at Punjab Engineering College in Chandigarh.

I met Kabir Sharma during the counselling session, and we became roommates in Vindhya hostel. He was a tall, slightly overweight, very fair-complexioned, strictly vegetarian guy, hardly the kind of person who would become my buddy for life. Ketan, a good-looking, muscular guy was our third roommate. He came from a rich business family of Ludhiana.

First semester took ignition, both in academics and co-curricular.

'Inter College Techno Fest', the most awaited event was round the corner. The college corridors had started buzzing with the preparations.

Sitting on the stairs, next to the college lawns, the discussion about the hottest event of the festival was on.

"Ashwin, so what are the plans for Made for Each Other (MFEO) contest?" Kabir sounded keen to know.

A smile was my only response.

The MFEO contest was the most desired and delicious icing that crowned the fest. Almost every senior worth his salt was living a dream of asking Chandani of first year Electrical, easily the most beautiful girl in college, to become his partner.

During the first break that morning, there were about sixty students standing near the canteen, enjoying hot samosas with tea. Our batch was dressed up in khakis as we had our workshop on that day. Hundred-and-twenty eyes forgot to blink and half the number of hearts stopped to beat as Chandani catwalked towards the canteen. The spell was cast. Her stirring presence made the crowd immobile till she came and stood in front of me.

"Ashwin from Mechanical first year?" A soft voice oozed out of her lips.

A personified enigma was by my side. I had heard her description several times over and seen her from a distance, but . . . but . . . to see her in flesh and blood so near, that too addressing me, that too by my name, I had it and more than me the boys had it.

"Yes, I am. And you?" I quizzed deliberately. I realised that for the first time in my life, I had failed to ditch my nervousness. She smiled but chose not to reply to my question, with an expression of 'how dare you, know me not'.

"You will be my partner in the MFEO Contest," she commanded. Without waiting for my response, she smiled, turned, and walked away, leaving me speechless.

"You will never get the girl you dream of . . ." Pandit *Anand Sharma's words echoed in my ears and an ironical smile melanged at my lips with the sip of coffee.*

The news spread like a wildfire in the campus. Everyone was realigning one's polarity based on this news. I became an object of envy. First-year Mechanical was especially happy at my triumph.

We apparently made a great couple. She was beauty with brains, and I was almost a match to her in both of them. Fair, five-ten, sparkling eyes, well-dressed, witty, caring, thoughtful, and simply lovable. With our combined strengths, we could have won the contest hands down.

Alas! Truancies of destiny weave their own patterns. That night, a sobbing Ketan approached me and said, "Please don't pair up with Chandani."

His face looked as if he had just heard the pronouncement of unpardonable banishment from Caesar. Like a true friend I nipped my budding love story with a heavy heart and moved out of the contest.

My sacrifice, however, went without rewards for Ketan, as Chandani went on to win the contest next day with my replacement from third-year Mechanical. Everyone clapped in the auditorium except two pairs of hands.

In order to get over the frustration of the evening, we all went to watch a festival special in our college auditorium where the movies were screened by the gang of Projection Club. A three-hour movie generally lasted for six hours due to the *masala* scenes being repeated time and again, on request. The movie had started when we walked in.

"Vikas *oye*," Kabir shouted loudly.

Immediately, we heard a guiding chorus from the Mech bunch as we wriggled our way through the darkness.

"Repeat *oye*," Vikas shouted as he eagerly informed us that we had just missed a rather hot scene. The projection guys immediately acceded to the request.

"Cheers to the tragic heroes of Mechanical," Vikas said and clandestinely passed us a glass of rum and cola. After a couple of big sips the glass got snatched out of our hands.

While watching the movie, I was haunted by the Chandani debacle as I looked at Ketan sitting next to me. The two could-have-beens found solace in rum cola, the supply of which was quite generous.

Everyone hooted and danced, with all those ecstatic moves and grooves, along with the heroine at every 'repeat'.

We returned to our hostel at three in the morning after watching a seven-hour movie. The combined purging effect of movie and rum had led to the cleansing of ceremonial defilement caused by MFEO contest.

"More coffee for you, sir?" Jack asked. I still had a smile on my lips as I looked up. Fluttering my eyes, I said, "One more please".

The rain had picked up slightly and I could hear the thunder in the distance. I looked up at the TV screen on the far right corner of the cafe and noticed that our cricket team was doing rather poorly.

"Rahu effect on the team!" I smiled sarcastically and then stopped halfway as I was reminded of a very funny situation.

It was the finals of the inter-hostel cricket match being played with tennis balls. We were in second year and were based in Himalaya hostel. The final was against Aravalli. One tip catch out was a rule in our competition. We had engineered several such rules so as to make the game more interesting.

The equation was very simple. Three balls left, two wickets in hand with two to win. Khullar, our star bowler, wearing his lucky red T-shirt, was bowling. As he sent a well-planned *tappa* ball, asking to be a hit out of the arena, the batsman could not contain his excitement as he saw the slow ball bouncing and coming to him at a very strike worthy length and in his excitement, hit it much harder than the law of physics demanded.

The ball went miles up in the air before it reached a point where its velocity became zero – we had solved some similar application problems last night – and then gathered momentum as it came down towards the mid wicket, where a bottom-heavy, bespectacled, utterly buttery R P Singh was moving his buttocks, not his legs, to and fro and was getting ready to take the catch. I realised, standing at the slips, that the way he was cupping his hands, he had probably forgotten that a direct catch was a not-out, and I started rushing towards him shouting loudly.

While the ball was having a bird's-eye view of the entire proceedings below, the batsmen were no less confused as the non- striker completed the run while the striker still had his eyes on the ball.

As the former screamed at the latter to take the two winning runs, both the batsmen were stranded at the strikers' end and in confusion, both of them started running towards the non-striker, now both having their eyes on the ball. In the meantime, Khullar, realising that R. P. Singh was going to take a direct catch, also came charging like a bull towards him, yelling at the top of his voice. As the ball inched towards the hands of R. P. Singh, his posterior moved left and right even faster with absolutely no foot movement. Due to Khullar's last-minute jump, the ball bounced right on the forehead of R. P. Singh and got lobbed towards me. I was rushing in from the slip region and had almost reached R. P. Singh, who now lay prostrate on the ground, when I caught the ball after a bounce. In the melee, both the batsmen, after running like headless chickens, were stranded in the middle. In one single action I threw the ball at the non-striker's end. There was nobody backing up.

If I had missed . . . But I did not. We had taken two wickets with one ball as was legal by our rules. But no one realised that it was illegal for a fielder to cross the pitch, which I had done unwittingly.

"Game over," I yelled sitting on the top of the hapless R. P. Singh while the rest piled on top of me.

"Struggling, failed, frustrated me . . . " The Pandit's words were an anticlimax to my experiences.

"Well done, Ashwin! That was quick thinking," complimented Vivek Bahman. He was a third year Metallurgy student who was playing the role of our coach. He was famous for his wit, the quality which was instrumental in getting him the appointment of the chief editor of *The Peckers*, the college magazine. He had a sharp eye for all sports but was only an *outstanding* performer and never a part of the team. He made a good coach though.

We gathered for a celebration in Bahman's room. He brought out two bottles of Old Monk from his huge tin case, God knows where he got his supplies from, and poured them in the trophy trough and then proceeded to add various juices to the concoction. There was a bright gleam in his eyes as he watched his masterpiece, the rum punch.

"This looks good," the unsuspecting teetotaller Kabir said as he walked into the room.

"Try then," offered Bahman with a mischievous smile. Before I could warn him, Kabir had already gulped down the first glass.

"Another one?" asked Bahman

This time even my pre-warning went waste.

Our mess cooks had prepared *bada khana* that night to celebrate our success. Kabir, sitting next to me, was singing loudly, all by himself.

"He sings when he is happy," remarked Ketan.

"He is triply happy today then," quipped the witty Bahman from across the table.

"I want a chicken meal," I could hear Kabir say. I was surprised because supposedly, he was a pure vegetarian.

"Let him taste it once," Bahman said, indicating to me to stay put.

Well, Bahman was so right. He liked it so much that every Monday, Wednesday, and Friday, when chicken curry was served in the mess, Kabir virtually stood up on his seat, shouting at the waiter to give him a "breast piece". He had since been nicknamed as "the breast piece."

"Your coffee, sir," the waiter said as I was still lost in Kabir's antics at the dinner table.

I took a long savouring sip and looked around. The café had a very colonial setting with very classy ambience, sofas with big armrests, imposing pictures, very stylish crockery, and soft music. Even the waiter looked like the traditional English butler, dressed in white-and-black tail suit. I could see through the giant window, the water poodles slowly forming on the walkway. A wave swept me off to my past again.

"Water is drying up in the Sukhna Lake. There is a *Shramdaan* camp coming up to save Sukhna. We need to participate in the camp big time," I was speaking to the members of the Drama Club. I had been elected secretary of the club and had included social service activities in our agenda.

"I want volunteers," I said.

Almost thirty hands went up.

Then Leena, from first year civil, who had earlier been crowned as Ms Fresher and had been an automatic choice for the Drama Club, put her hand up slowly. She was, I summarised, a habitually late reactor.

The remaining twenty hands went up instantly.

"Some things never change," I muttered.

Ms Leena had a blushing smile on her face. I realised she was not dumb, she was perhaps trying to figure out her popularity.

We spent almost seven afternoons digging up the lake, along with several other citizens of Chandigarh. We were working in the areas near the Lake Club. Since most of the better-looking girls in our college were in our club and almost each one was helping out now, the army of the unwanted volunteers from PEC grew at a rapid pace.

"Some tea for you, sir?" I heard Leena addressing me from the bank while I was digging below.

I looked at her with a short question in my eyes.

"My father is a member of this club," she explained.

She had an army of three waiters in attendance, each one carrying a tray. I could make out that she was trying to impress me.

"Come down, Leena, we have a job to finish," I commanded.

She reluctantly picked up a shovel and started filling the steel container. From nowhere, three pairs of hands appeared and whisked away the silt-filled container, all from first year civil, I presumed.

"See the power of leveraging," I grinned into Kabir's ears.

Kabir, in the meantime, had dug out a pile load of plastic bags.

I looked at him disgustedly and said, "What you reap is what you sow. This is the major culprit and still some people never learn."

Kabir was on the defensive when he slowly replied, "As per *upayas,* feeding water creatures helps pacify your malevolent stars. There is nothing wrong in this."

"Goddamn! It is plastic. You are killing water by doing so and the very creatures you are trying to feed," I retorted back. Kabir just kept digging quietly.

I knew Kabir believed in astrology a lot and had visited several *pandits* to seek the ways of attaining goals, material or immaterial. He was religiously involved in doing *upayas* and wearing clothes as per colour of the day. Everybody knew that he was going through the phase of *Shanni Dhaiya*. He had already proclaimed to everyone that based on his horoscope predictions, he would work for five years in a private company after passing out and then would be involved in teaching throughout his life, just like his father. Although I was a very rational person, my friendship with Kabir had grown because he was very reliable, honest, and a true friend.

The four years of engineering passed rather quickly. Ketan finished college on a high, coming out tops in the project. I was placed in the top three, and Kabir didn't do badly either. I joined the MBA Programme in Panjab University Campus while Kabir stayed put and joined master's programme in Punjab Engineering College. He was on cloud nine because not only had he got an adhoc job in the college, he was also going to teach Sabeeha. He always had a crush on her.

***

Being in the MBA department was a beautiful phase of my life. Nestled between the English department on left and Law on right, it was just at a stone's throw from the Student Centre, the heart of University.

The first semester passed off in hard work as the subjects were very different. I topped that term in the Marketing section, and Kabir's compliments were all reserved for my stars rather than my hard work. We began to relax a little more as we entered the second semester.

For the summer training project, I had to do market research for a company in Rajasthan. After forty-five days, we submitted the report and received our first payment, a handsome stipend, and we were very thrilled.

The university was coming back to life as we came back.

"Nancy is joining MPM," Nitin shouted as he came running with the hot news. She was probably, the hottest babe to join the department that year. Nitin had done his summer training in the department itself and was privy to the interviews that had taken place.

"She is so beautiful, *yaar*," he gushed.

Probably, what he meant was that he was already half in love and was kind of requesting others to stay away. But like hounds smelling blood, everyone surrounded Nitin for vital bites. There was an all-around feel-good factor, and Nitin in particular was behaving like an electron in a high state of excitement.

"Will someone teach me mathematics?" I heard Nancy requesting to the group.

It was her first day in the department and her second lecture had been that of maths, apparently her Achilles' heel. We were sitting on the steps during the break when I heard her pleading. Almost everyone surrounded her as I sat back, lost in my own thoughts. Everyone was eager to help her. Everyone accompanied her to the canteen in the back, where they offered her tea, *samosas,* and free advice.

I met her for the first time, later in the day during the lunch break, as she walked into our class. I was there, all by myself, waiting for two of my friends to return from the mess.

"Chic and pretty, an absolute cut-out for these two words," I thought as I looked at her. She was dressed in well-fitted blue jeans, a smart off-white shirt, and blue sneakers, with a large brown bag hanging by her side. She had her long hair tied up nicely, with some falling on her face, just the way I love.

She shifted on her legs before she asked, "Are you in MBA II?"

I nodded curtly without speaking out.

"My name is Nancy. I am in first year MPM, and I am looking for Ashwin," words cascaded from her lips softly, almost like a gingerly flowing spring.

"Why are you looking for Ashwin?" I asked, as though surprised, admiring the dimples on her face which made her look very cute.

"I believe he is the topper, and I want to take his help in Maths." she spoke hesitantly.

"Have you asked him?" I questioned her with a playful smile.

"No, not yet. But I am here to speak to him," she replied, as she looked towards the door. I picked my bag and walked out of the class. At the door I turned and said, "Ashwin will not teach you."

I walked to the canteen and ordered tea.

"What is this happening to me? I am not so rude," I thought as I closed my eyes.

"Ashwin you can wake up now," I heard Nancy's voice. The canteen boy had placed two cups of tea on the table.

"I know you did not have any lunch and you can't say no because my mom makes excellent food," she said with a beautiful smile on her face and took out her lunch box. I could not help liking her as I gave in. Besides, I was hungry.

"The food is really good," I remarked, savouring the mouthful.

"I will get lunch for you every day, if you promise to teach me," she bartered.

I looked at her face for about good thirty seconds and thought, "She does not need an MBA degree to learn marketing."

"I am a tough taskmaster," I said. Her face broke into a broad grin. Her cheeks looked chubby on her petite frame.

She was like a breath of fresh air in my life. We became good friends instantly. I made her work hard, and she proved to be a quick learner. Although I had not yet compartmentalised my feelings for her, rumours were ripe in the department in advance. To be honest, sitting on the stairs, which was our favourite pastime when not studying, without her, made my heart lonely.

"So, here you are," I could hear Kabir's voice that transferred me to reality. He had come looking for me in the Willow Café. Both Kabir and I had joined the same start up company at Chandigarh after passing out. We had together rented an apartment in Sector 11.

"I was waiting for you in the apartment. Since you got late I came looking for you here. Had dinner?" he asked without waiting for my reply.

"Not yet. I didn't feel like eating," I replied.

"What did Panditji say?" he asked while looking at the menu.

I did not reply.

"Let us have some sandwiches, Okay?" he suggested. He placed the order and then looked at me expectantly.

I took a deep breath as I relaxed on the sofa with my feet stretched and hands folded behind my head, gave him a verbatim report of my visit to Panditji's office. Kabir's smiling face was anxiousness personified by the time my story finished. He took a glass of water, drank it in one go, and thumped it onto the table.

He was perhaps gathering his thoughts as he sat on the edge of his seat, his body bent forward, his jaw resting in his hands, and his elbows on his thighs. I looked at him, awaiting his reaction. The momentary silence was puzzling.

He finally spoke in a rather grave voice, pronouncing his verdict, "My God! You are going to be in the clutches of Rahu for the next eighteen years."

My nostalgic trip down the memory lane in the last few hours had smoothened my nerves by this time. I was back to my usual confident self.

"Rahu, uh . . . rubbish," I retorted.

Kabir sank back into his seat, shrugged his shoulders, and exhaled deeply. He knew it would be difficult to convince me, still he continued, "You have to believe, Ashwin. Astrology is a science which has been practiced by our sages and even the greatest of mathematicians."

I straightened my posture, put my hand up, signalling him to stop, and said, "He just wants to make money by selling his Rahu stuff."

Kabir got up and walked towards the window with arms folded in front. He looked out into the clouded night sky, pitying my ignorance about the approaching storm, turned back, and spoke sympathetically, "I have known him for many years now. His predictions have always been accurate."

"I don't believe in this. In fact, I am angry with myself for going there," I replied.

Kabir walked towards me, raised his eyebrows, and spoke in a nervous voice, "You cannot ignore the fact that your mahadasa of negatively placed Rahu has just started. You are in for tough times, buddy."

I knew he meant well. He had faith in his belief and I had in mine. I held his hand, patted his rather wet palm, and made him sit by my side. The calmness of my speech was to soothen his nerves. "It is all in the mind, Kabir. Panditji has to dramatise and exaggerate situations so as to make money out of the gullible."

He continued to look into my eyes silently as I carried on, "If I have to struggle, I will. Isn't life full of struggle? Wasn't engineering full of struggle? If your Rahu does induce setbacks, then let my success be judged by how I bounce back. If he creates problems, I will find solutions. How? I don't know, but succeed I will."

Kabir had to take out a tissue and wipe off his face. He was clearly anxious, and some unknown eerie fright was lurking in his eyes. It was he who seemed to be in the clutches of Rahu, not me.

"Only Panditji's remedies can save you now. Please do them religiously," he sounded both lost and concerned at the same time.

I stood up tall in front of Kabir, with my jaws clenched as I took out the paper, on which Panditji had apparently plotted my defence against Rahu, and tore it into half. I kept on tearing it into halves till the time I couldn't do it any further. I still remember how each tear had lent me a feel of emancipation that day. I felt I had been able to wrench the smoky blue millstone of Rahu off my back.

I still remember how light and calm I had felt after that.

Sitting in my aisle seat in the plane, I heaved a long sigh. Even now I could feel the calm that had descended on me as I had decided to fight back. My fight with *Panditji's Rahu* had started nine years back and continued till this day. Somewhere in the gypsy's words lay solution to the apparition blueth. I scanned through the last few years of my fight with Rahu, looking for clues to solve the riddles.

A period of Rahu in Rahu . . . You will be chasing dreams unsuccessfully . . . will flatter to deceive . . . change in job . . . very ambitious . . . no stability . . . mind easily misled.

Astro speaks

Chapter 4

Rahu Strikes

The ring was ready. The gong struck and the fight was on. The noises from all around lent boost to the fighting spirits of both the warriors. It was no less than the bout of boxing between an elf and a behemoth.

The giant Rahu, wearing blue boxer shorts, going well with his light-blue toned physique, dark blue gloves over his jumbo fists, was in the blue corner. His gladiator-like ferocious looks were laden with an extraordinary confidence originating from his natural supremacy. There was a cunning grin on his lips and a deadly mischief in his eyes which seemed to be echoing, "Look for an escape route, buddy."

I was in the red corner. Guided by my perseverance, I was ready to play the mental game on a physical platform. The skies were dusty and musty red. The hissing of the approaching storm took away my attention for a while. The fury of sound captured all my senses but an incredible grit got induced and the fighter in me rose to counter the punches. I could see amongst the audience, the pleading eyes of Kabir, waiting for my surrender and the bewitching eyes of Panditji, as if calling me a fool.

Irrespective of the immeasurable might of my dreaded enemy *Rahu*, I proceeded on to my date with life, leaving behind Kabir's confidence in the stars far away and his love and concern for me, so close to his heart. I moved on with my fight in the arena of life.

After leaving the department, I worked for three months in an engineering exports company in Chandigarh, where Kabir had also joined. But within a couple of months, I received my appointment letter from a Russian multinational company based in Delhi. A wave of glee swept through me.

I had won round one, against my unusual rival. Kabir was proven wrong. Panditji, who had announced Rahu as a natural winner, too was proven wrong, and a smile rolled over my whistling lips.

I moved to Delhi, the city which provides an easy refuge to fresh-from-the-garden MBAs. I shared a flat with two of my friends, who were already working in Delhi. I travelled to my office with my roommate Ajay, as we worked in the adjoining buildings.

My boss, Mr Rosnoski, about fifty years of age, was a human encyclopaedia, and so I had developed tremendous respect for him. He was in India, overseeing the imports and marketing of products from Russia. He was very fit for his age although he was a chain smoker.

Within a month of my joining, I had learnt the nuances of the trade. I worked hard, read a lot, and more importantly, observed a lot.

Mr Rosnoski was quite pleased with my extra initiatives. One day he called me in his office and said, "Ashwin, get your passport tomorrow as you now need to spend some time in our St. Petersburg office. We need to apply for your visa."

I was very happy naturally, as I thought about that beautiful city located on Neva River by the Baltic Sea. I was humming softly to myself, oblivious of the fact that *Rahu was ready to punch back, not once but twice.*

Roads of Delhi were quite wide and welcoming around Connaught Place, the location of my office. I was returning home, pillion-riding on my friend Ajay's bike on a Saturday evening. October breeze was as pleasant as Indian West wind, a time of beautiful days, a season that demands warmth, as offered by a passionate romance.

Before I could relish this bliss further, all of a sudden I saw a big animal running towards me and hit me hard.

"Aaa . . . Aaahhh!" These creepy sounds emerged from my mouth as I went up in the air and landed with a thud.

"Ashwin . . . Ash . . . win," I could hear a faint, familiar voice of Ajay, reverberating as if in a big empty earthen pot. "Are you all right? Oh, you are bleeding."

I could hear everything, see everything, but somehow all my senses simply refused to respond.

"Rahu's punch," I uttered and smiled sarcastically to myself even in severe pain. We were thronged by passers-by. Some genuinely wanted to help and for some, I was an object of discussion.

Myriad comments were making rounds, bordering from concern to insanity.

"Beta, you must donate mustard oil on Saturday to keep *Shani Maharaj* happy," somebody from Kabir's clan spoke out loud.

Fortunately, I could get up in one piece. Ajay, who was untouched during this mayhem, took me to a doctor.

"Ligament tear," the doctor pronounced as he advised me to take bed rest for ten days.

"Your back seems quite intoxicating, as the bull lost his senses the moment he saw you," Ajay chuckled.

I couldn't help but smile.

As I tried to get up from bed, I realised that my body was hurting at more places than one. I hopped to the washroom with Ajay's help. Against the doctor's advice, I wanted to get back to work, as my first overseas trip beckoned.

Just then, I heard the phone ring.

"Hello, this is Ajay," I could hear Brar's voice.

"Hi, Kabir! How are you this morning?" I heard him again.

Ajay was still gossiping with Kabir as I limped back, dragging my right foot. As I sat in the chair, he passed the phone to me.

"Hello, Kabir . . ." I grimaced.

"I told you that *Panditji* is always right. He had very clearly predicted an accident for you," he half cried, half shouted at me.

"This was just a petty accident. These things do happen," I gave my logic. "Moreover, I am doing so well here that my boss has asked me to go to our St Petersburg office." My words were well clad with confidence. It was *my* defence against *his Rahu*. "Count ten, buddy. I'll be on my feet before that," I chuckled.

Kabir, unmoved by my defence, continued in the same vein, "Listen, Ashwin, you have to appease *Rahu Maharaj* or else you will suffer. You please do the *upayas*. I will talk to *Panditji* again and will call you back in the evening."

Standing by the ringside, Kabir pleaded me to concede the bout to the boxer in blue.

He put the phone down without waiting for my reply.

Ajay dropped me at the office. As I signed in, the receptionist asked me to see Mr Rosnoski in his cabin.

As I walked into his room, I could sense that something was not okay. Mr Rosnoski was rather grim-faced that morning, and the half-full ashtray showed that he had already smoked half a dozen cigarettes by then.

"We are closing down Indian operations," he came straight to the point.

"But why?" I was zapped.

"Yesterday, the government changed import policies and nullified our special agreement of zero duty," he explained to me.

I felt disgusted.

"You can move with me to Russia if you want. You are a good lad, and I am sure you will grow with us," he offered.

A polite decline was the only option since I had no intention of settling down permanently in a foreign land. So, I thanked him for his offer and walked out. I was going to be jobless by the end of that week. The only good thing was that Mr Rosnoski had assured all of us six months' salary.

Kabir called again that night. I signalled Ajay to tell him that I had gone off to sleep. I knew my latest problem would charge him further, to prove his *Panditji* right. Ajay, however, gave a brief description about the day's happening, to which Kabir responded with a long monologue.

Ajay kept listening patiently with an odd *'oh'* and *'Achha!'* Finally, he put the phone down saying, "I will tell him, bye."

He settled comfortably on my bed and asked, "What do you intend to do now?"

I had no immediate plans for future, so I kept quiet.

He spoke after a while, "Kabir's *Panditji* wants you to do some remedies immediately or else you will suffer more. There won't be any stability and you may move away from motherland."

I could see myself in the ring, lying on the floor, bleeding. I raised my sweat-heavy eyelids to look for the rope as support. I lifted my body, shook my head, and got up on my feet, looking right into the eyes of the blue demon.

"Who says I am suffering? Look, the accident was a minor one. Today, I have more money than what you guys will earn over the next six months. I believe I am doing quite okay. I have already learnt the tricks of the trade. Getting a new job wouldn't be a problem for me," I retorted, punching *Panditji*'s nose in my mind.

"Instead of moving away from motherland, I will now go back home and get a decent job there," I continued. I felt very relaxed.

The following week, I was back in Jalandhar. Barring my injury, my parents were happy to see me back. I was almost kind of rich, for the time being, enough to buy nice gifts for everyone at home and also to buy a second-hand car. I was generally feeling good except that I had to look for a good job. My choice was limited as I was looking only at export-based companies.

Kabir came home the following Sunday morning. The bear hug he gave me addressed his care for me.

I was feeling very good that day as I took Kabir out for dinner at the newly opened *Kebab Factory* at Radisson. We ordered Kingfisher Light beer to go with Kebabs. Kabir soon got nostalgic about Sabeeha and needed my assurance that she would be an ideal wife for him. He had still not proposed to her.

"What are you waiting for? You have done your master's, have a job too. She will be passing out this year. Propose to her before her parents fix up her marriage elsewhere," I said seriously, remembering my case.

Kabir nodded. We went silent for a few minutes.

"Any new girl in your life?" he asked, looking at me, quite aware of the fact that Nancy's sudden arranged marriage had created a void in my life.

"If only I had reaction time," I thought as I gulped down my drink. I was waiting for Kabir's comment that *Rahu* had been instrumental in my suffering, but thankfully it never came.

He again went quiet for a few minutes. He deliberately distracted me very intelligently, "Did you meet anyone interesting in Delhi?"

"Not in Delhi, but someone in *Pandit* Anand Sharma's office," I replied with a naughty smile on my lips. Once the Pandora's box opened, Kabir ensured that he got complete details of the girl I had met there.

Her thoughts stayed with me till I went off to sleep that night.

The next morning came with a ray of hope for me. There was a very interesting advertisement in the newspaper. The managing director of Avin International, who had also been elected as the chairman of Engineering Exports Promotion Council of India, had advertised for the post of executive assistant to the MD, almost a shadow MD, if you played your cards right.

That Wednesday, I reached Ludhiana where the walk-in interview was to be conducted. As I walked into their corporate office, I was surprised to see more than fifty candidates waiting in queue for a single post. As I wouldn't have got my turn by night, a thought struck and I scribbled a note on a piece of paper, walked up to Mr Verma, the PA, and requested him to pass on the note to the MD.

He looked at the slip and murmured, "Mr Ashwin . . ." and walked in as the bell rang.

I wasn't surprised when I was the next person to be called in. My interview lasted for almost an hour. There were no further interviews after mine. I was asked to join immediately at double the salary. Mr Verma rushed to congratulate me when I walked out and quizzed, "What did you write on that slip, sir?"

I was glad to note that I had graduated to sir from Mr Ashwin in just one hour. I scribbled on Mr Verma's notepad,

"If you do not call me in now, your loss will be greater than mine."

Mr G. P. Singhania or GP in short, was an awe-inspiring personality. He was chairing very prestigious positions on a pan-India basis. Interestingly, both of us had a showdown on day one itself. GP, who had come back from Delhi that morning, wanted to discuss the exports article on page three of *The Economic Times*.

I very confidently said, "There is no such article in today's paper, sir."

He stared at me and said, "Don't you think, my boy, confidence carried a bit too far becomes overconfidence."

I picked up the day's paper, opened page three and with a triumphant smile on my face, said, "This is Chandigarh edition, sir, while you are carrying Delhi edition."

Most employees shivered to meet him and here I was, practically eating out of his hand on the very first day.

Avi, from the product development department, was a nice-looking guy with a well-trimmed beard. He was in charge of Far East market and had developed a very fine reputation. I often shared his sumptuous home-cooked lunch. He became a good friend, almost my mentor for the years to come.

My usual catharsis was to drive down to Chandigarh almost every alternate weekend. Kabir called me one Friday afternoon and asked, "Are you coming tomorrow?"

"Yes, I am," I said enthusiastically.

"Let us go to Kasauli tomorrow evening. I am going to book a cottage there. Fine with you?" he asked.

"Oh yes! We will pick up beer from Panchkula and chicken pickle from *Dhalli*. I will pick you up at 4 p.m. Okay?" I shot back and hung up as Mr Verma came looking for me.

Friday evening, we were on our way to Kasauli. The winters were setting in. As we touched the Shimla road, a mild chill in the breeze caressed my face when I lowered the window pane. The beauteous perfection of nature was at its best. Land was rising gracefully as if stretching out in laze to form hills. The landscape was laden with luscious green trees, swaying gently to add on to the mystery of their woody aroma. There was a big crowd going towards Shimla that evening which slowed us down. We picked up speed after crossing Dharampur *chowk*.

I could sense that Kabir had something on his mind which was itching to come out.

"Seems like old times," he remarked. I nodded in affirmation.

Kasauli, a small hilly town short of Shimla, had been our regular jaunt during our college days. Marked by old colonial cottages, Kasauli had a strange air of romance and peace. Perhaps, it was Nancy's favourite song which was playing on the FM channel, which opened the floodgates of memory.

I still remember it was 5 p.m. on a cold December evening. I was talking to Nancy on our university hostel phone.

"So you care for me," she teased.

"I can do anything for you," I said.

"I love Kasauli's bun-samosa," she giggled and put the phone down, almost test- teasing me.

I ran back to Brar's room, where he was lying snuggled in his bed. He was sleeping in my favourite deep-blue pullover. But this was no time to complain as I yanked off his quilt and asked him to come with me.

After half an hour's drive, I realised that our bike's headlight was not working. I silently cursed Puneet who had borrowed my bike last night. Brar was firmly ensconced on the back seat with his arms around me. He had wrapped himself in a big shawl and had a smug look on his face, although his teeth were chattering with cold. Thankfully, I was wearing a warm jacket. By the time we reached Kasauli and picked up bun-samosas and gulab jamuns from the famous Tannu halwai's shop on a walk-only paved road just above the bus stand, it had become very foggy.

"What the hell am I doing out here?" Brar didn't say but his face did . . .

We somehow managed to reach back in one piece. I went to Sector 36 market and called her from Archie's shop, which was right outside her house. I asked her to come out for a moment.

All my cold disappeared the moment I saw her. I handed over the packet to her and drove away. Her bewildered face was worth millions to me . . . .

"Pick up some speed, *bhai*," Kabir interrupted.

"Indeed, seems like old times, except that old times are missing," I spoke softly, lost in my own world.

We drove up the romantic hills of Kasauli, full of nostalgic thoughts. The air was fresh and cool, the pine trees were majestic, and the lights peeping out of small log huts looked beautiful. Kasauli was just like a vintage wine, simply intoxicating. I could live there forever.

Our cottage, a part of a reasonably good property, turned out to be a cute little log hut. We sat in the back verandah which had a magnificent view of the valley below. There were stars twinkling above in the sky and far below in the valley too. We took out our chilled beer from the cold storage box and started savouring the *Dhalli* speciality chicken pickle with bread.

"I have some news for you," Kabir said.

I looked at him questioningly.

"Her name is Manvi!" He announced secretively, as if he had let out a Swiss bank account number.

"So have you broken up with Sabeeha?" I quizzed.

Paying no heed to my comment, he continued, "She is also going through a period of *Rahu maha dasa*, like you. She had come to *Panditji* with her mother."

My thoughts rushed back to *Panditji's* waiting area, as I vividly recollected her charming face.

"Oh!" was all that I could say.

"Her parents were looking for a match for her at that time. That's why her mother brought her to *Panditji*. But her first marriage was going to be turbulent as per *Panditji*," Kabir explained.

Seeing that I was in a listening mode, Kabir pressed his luck. "The placement of *Rahu* in her house of marriage would result in a separated life for her."

"So your *Panditji* did not suggest any remedies to her," I asked sarcastically.

"Now I understand why she looked gloomy as she had walked out of *Panditji's* room that day," I thought.

"*Panditji* had given her a list of things to do. If she had done them, then she could have got relief," he replied.

How could such a pretty young thing suffer so much? I felt my heart reaching out to her as I said, "And what is the guarantee that what your *Pandit* says, will happen?"

"It has already happened. *Panditji* is always right," Kabir said authoritatively.

I was listening very keenly to him.

"She had got married, a month after you saw her, to an NRI from the USA. She returned home the same night, as her husband already had a live-in relationship, back in Chicago. She is now separated but not divorced, just as *Panditji* had predicted," he explained.

Honestly, I had mixed feelings. I was sad for her but somewhere felt relaxed within. I didn't know why.

There was a momentary silence as we refilled our glasses.

Kabir continued with his star talk, "Horoscope reading and forecasting is a science and has been practiced in India for ages. Even well-known scientists and mathematicians practice astrology. *Panditji* just studies the movement of different planets and forecasts events based on mathematical calculations."

My problems were the least of my concern as I chuckled, "I look forward to seeing Mr *Rahu*."

"Look, Ashwin, you are blessed with a strong mind and you will not appreciate my concerns. Had you done the remedies, you might have been in a better position than what you are in now. Think about people like Manvi, who are now struggling and suffering. After all, a hammer that forges steel also shatters glass," argued Kabir.

This was perhaps the most convincing argument Kabir had ever made in his life. The very thought of the delicate Manvi getting shattered like a piece of glass by *Rahu* had struck the innermost chord of my heart.

"Where is she?" I asked.

"She is working as a journalist in Chandigarh," replied Kabir feeling a little more important.

There was a knock at the door. As we had ordered, a delivery boy from Dharampur's dhaba had brought us our favourite *paranthas* and *egg bhurji*. The conversation during dinner moved on to Sabeeha. I slept at 2 a.m. with thoughts of Manvi. Her plight had touched my heart somewhere.

A few weeks later, I got a call from Kabir. "I am worried about you," he said in a shade quieter tone.

"What happened?" I queried.

"*Panditji* has predicted high level of dissatisfaction, frustration and changes in your career and problems in your love life," he spoke in a grave voice.

Kabir struck the gong again as he presented a woeful picture of the shape of things to come.

"I will take care of *Rahu*. Don't worry," I retorted.

"You put one coconut with one kg black lentil in river every Saturday," he almost begged.

I laughed and said, "Just let me know whenever there is any news of Manvi."

The following month I flew to Singapore along with Avi. We had developed an excellent relationship by then. He was a modern-day avatar of Chanakaya. He was, what you say, a true friend and was both rustic and polished at the same time.

We were having lunch at Joo Chiat Place the next day. The working lunch served on a banana leaf, consisted of rice, chicken masala spread on the top, two fried potatoes, salad, and juice. The food was steaming, tasty, and served very hygienically, just the way I liked.

"I have something important to discuss," he said.

I looked at him inquisitively.

"I have been approached by Mr Gupta of Every Day Tools to market their products in South East and Far East Asia. We need a professional to be based in Singapore for about six months to set things up here. The money is very good if you are interested to join," he explained.

It was now his turn to look at me curiously.

I nodded as I had started trusting Avi like an elder brother. If Avi wanted me in, I knew I would go ahead. I had nothing to lose but lots to gain, more international experience as I would be travelling often to neighbouring countries. I had to be away from home but only for six months.

That evening, I had my first encounter with beer in Singapore. Avi ordered pitchers for us. They were huge. It took me an hour to finish one and could have no more while Avi calmly finished his third.

I marvelled at myself as I was getting accustomed to good luck.

"If this is what a bad Rahu does, I wonder what a good one does," I smiled and told myself as I went to bed that night, mentally sparring with Rahu. I was actually smiling and singing simultaneously, as I focused my energy on a strong knockout punch.

I pulled my gloved right hand all the way back and made a 'whoosh' sound to land my all-important punch on his jaws. The boxer in blue sidestepped, but the momentum of my missed punch landed me on the bed.

It was a happy knockout for me, fully helped by the happy hours' beer, as I entered the world of sleep.

Two months later, I was back in Singapore. I worked hard for the next three months, and we had started building a good market for our products.

Surprisingly, I got a fax from Avi one morning, "Come back, Ashwin. We are closing down Singapore office."

I immediately dialled his number and asked, "What happened, Avi?"

He replied in a heavy voice, "The government has changed incentive scheme and our products have become non-competitive. So wind up and fly back asap."

Rahu had left me with a swollen black eye. I wondered whether he was onto fight until my death to please the spectators!

We had a meeting with Mr Gupta back in office in India. Mr Gupta was a very straightforward but a generous man. He was one-in-a-million kind of a man who took responsibility for the future of his associates.

"We are together in whatever we do. Let us grow together," he remarked.

As a habitual winner I could see myself rising again, this time without even the support of the rope of the ring. We used to sit in a ten-by-ten room making and implementing plans. The sound of a fax machine rolling out purchase orders in the form of a long white *sari* was perhaps the most cherished sound in our office. I distinctly remember the story of my first purchase order from the USA, rather vividly.

It was in October 2006 when I had first landed in USA.

Navi, my host, was a wonderful man and was working with Ford. I liked him instantly and wondered how similar Navi was to Avi. On Monday morning, he drove me from Detroit to Akron. We started at 2 a.m. and reached there by 5 a.m. Navi dropped me at a nearby "Little Boy" restaurant and rushed back to his office in Detroit. Unfortunately, the restaurant had not opened up and I had to wait in freezing cold.

The dawn was dusky and the air was heavy with vapours. I pulled my suitcase full of samples on the pebbled pathway and sat down on a bench next to the Little Boy's cut-out. The streetlights were desperate to spill out some light but the darkness seemed to be more domineering. The darkness slowly mélanged into a moist morning, as I sat waiting. I imagined that I had received huge orders from the customer and I smiled to myself. I was feeling cold, very cold and was almost shivering when I spotted the first headlight approaching. A motherly lady stepped out and opened the lock.

"Nice and early," she smiled at me. Her smile brought me warmth in that low-Fahrenheit time. I had learnt very quickly that these people would wish even strangers and were very civil.

I stuttered in my reply, entirely caused by my two hours' tryst with the cold. "I . . . I have been waiting for almost two hours, but thank you for asking."

"Come in and let me fix you a hot cup of coffee," she spoke tenderly as she held the door while I carried the case in. She gave me a blanket and fixed a steaming hot cup of coffee.

I had hardly known the lady till half an hour back. Yet her pleasant demeanour had brought me close to her. I ordered two eggs, sunny side up, toast, and a pot of tea as we continued to converse. The restaurant had filled up with grey-haired couples who had come there for breakfast. I was a little sad as I thanked her and walked out two hours later for my meeting.

"Our world could do a lot more with such compassionate people who help others without any strings attached," I thought to myself.

Maybe the universe was in unison with my thought of gratitude that morning. The cab driver who drove me down to the office was working part-time in Smartsell, where I had to go.

"I believe they are buying from an importer in Chicago. They are now looking for a direct source. You are here at just the right time, young fella," he informed.

In that imposing building, I crossed a row of offices before I entered the meeting room. The room had enormous glass windows overlooking a lush green lot. On one side, I could see the owner's Porsche shining in the sun's glory. There was an elegant product-display cabinet in the room. I laid out my samples on the centre table and waited for things to unfold.

Gary walked into the room after five minutes. He was wearing off-white flannels with a green golf shirt and a Nicholson hat. He was a handsome-looking man with slight stubble. He spoke in a heavily accented voice, "Hello, Ashwin, I am Gary."

He shook my hand vigorously. His pronunciation of 'i' in my name was as in wine, like most Americans do, and unlike as in 'win', which the British do. He whistled softly as he looked at the samples and I ascertained from his wide smile that he was sold on our product range and quality. I silently thanked our plating shop supervisor who had put an excellent, almost ornamental, gold finish on the samples.

I quietly opened my file and began filling up the pro forma invoice. I could hear Avi's voice ringing in my ears, "Always focus on getting a PI made before you get up from the table." We zeroed down to a total which Abir would have certainly considered as an auspiscious number. I was amazed that it had matched the number I had been visualising.

I requested them to fax a copy to our office in India. I knew everybody back home must be having their eyes on at the fax machine for the PO.

My reverie, which had brought a blissful smile on my face, was broken by the sirens of a police car. There was slight commotion outside as the police personnel barged into the building.

"Was the blue trying to sabotage my success?" I asked myself.

"Who dialled 911? What's going on?" the officer asked politely, ironically reminding me of the soft approach used back home under similar conditions.

911 is an emergency number in the USA. There was apparently some mix-up as no one had dialled this number from the building.

I figured out what might have happened, as I offered an explanation, "See, Officer, we were trying to send a fax to India with country code 91 followed by city code 161. Probably, the first three digits dialled together are causing this problem."

The officer looked appreciatively at me, shook hands with Gary, and walked away. "Always dial 011 to get on to the international line," I cautioned the purchase guy.

There was a good laugh all around.

***

During those days of struggle, Kabir constantly reminded me that *upayas* of *Rahu* were the only ointment for my brazen future.

One Sunday afternoon we were walking by Sukhna Lake. Kabir said, "By the way, *Panditji* has suggested me to change my name to Abir as 'A' works well with my horoscope."

"Oh, Kabir, please! What difference is this going to make to your life?" I was rather put off as I spoke.

"Plenty! For starters, Sabeeha has agreed to marry me. We will get married after five years though," he replied rather emphatically.

I hugged and congratulated him, "Wow! This is great news. But why wait for so long? And will she not marry you if you are Kabir?"

Ignoring my latter question, he replied, "My seventh house, which is the house of marriage, gets activated next year as per *Panditji*. But the negative aspect of *Rahu* finishes after five years and that is the most auspicious time for me to get married."

I threw my hands up in despair as he threw his final dice, "I have spoken to *Panditji* about your marriage also. If you want somebody in your life, you will have to do *upayas* of *Rahu*."

I smiled at his negotiating skills.

That night I had a weird dream. I saw Manvi in the claws of a demon shouting for help. I woke up with a start, full of sweat.

I was sweating even now, even in the cool confines of the aeroplane, as I remembered that dream.

My foe in blue seemed to have chalked out a cunning plan to knock me where it hurt the most. A beautiful trap was laid which no Eve, not even Manvi, could resist.

The lights in the plane had been switched off. Only a few reading lights were on. I covered myself with the blanket and remembered Rahu's cunning plan last year to let loose his most beguiling agent on Manvi.

Aimless travel . . . Ketu in Rahu will cause mental tension . . . will fall in love during period of Venus in Rahu . . . problem in love life . . . competitive environment

Astro speaks

Chapter 5

The Heat of Samar

Samar Taneja was a drop-dead gorgeous, irresistible, charismatic man who had women fawning all over him. He was involved in imports and distribution of medical equipment. Rich and famous, a mortal god of beauty, Samar was the chief speaker at a conference in Hotel Moore, Chandigarh, that evening.

Manvi, a freelance journalist was assigned the coverage of this conference. As she approached the parking lot, there wasn't any slot left.

She looked at her watch and exclaimed, "Gosh! I am already late. What to do?"

She parked her car near the exit, as it was the only area with some space left, and rushed towards the hotel. As she reached the gate, Manvi realised that she had forgotten her notepad in the car. This was so typical of her. Mumbling to herself, she half ran to retrieve it. Taking a deep breath, she chided herself and walked back to the conference venue.

Manvi, with a well-trimmed body in a peach chiffon sari, looked more desirable than any other cotton-clad spectacled journalist colleague of hers. Her brow had the traces of unworldly innocence rather than a worldly wisdom, unlike the people of her field. As she crossed the threshold, she looked around for a place to sit and heaved a sigh of relief to see a vacant chair in the first row.

"Excuse me, is this chair occupied?" she whispered to the person sitting next to it.

He looked at her. "No," an instant reply made its way out of his lips.

"Thanks," she said.

As she settled down, a deep imposing baritone filled the hall instantly, diverting her attention to the speaker. As she lifted her eyes, to her utter surprise, she felt as if the speaker was addressing her. To avoid that awkward encounter, she looked down at the pad and her notes picked up pace. She lifted up her heavy lashes again after a while. She almost went numb as Samar's gaze was still fixed on her. She tried to examine her *sari*, especially its pleats at the bottom. The fall was perfect. She glanced at her *pallu* and tried to put it in place, further expanding it over her bare arm and looked up again. Her notional impulse didn't cheat her this time. It was not spontaneous as he was still looking at her.

"Strange," she thought.

This time Manvi frowned but perhaps, her charming face was lacking the strength and solidity of annoyance as he didn't seem to be perturbed.

The impeccable presence of the speaker had left all the reporters speechless as he finished with his presentation.

"His wit and intelligence complemented his Greek-god-like persona," Manvi thought. But she wished him to be a gentleman too which she doubted he was.

The interesting question-answer session that followed, was brought to a sudden halt as a spark from an electric wire set ablaze the white satin fabric put up to adorn the wall behind the stage. Before the organisers could react, panic was let loose in the crowd.

"Please vacate the hall. Do not push, do not run," one of the organisers shouted on the mike. But people pushed and ran as the smoke filled in. The serene and orderly world of that room was a thing of past now.

The room got engulfed in darkness other than the yellow flickering glint of the flames. Suddenly, someone held her hand and guided her out.

"Are you okay? Are you all right?" Her almost fainted senses rose to this familiar sound, as he released her hand, though the familiarity was just four words old.

"Hi, I'm Abir," he said.

He was the same person sitting next to her in the hall.

"I'm fine," Manvi replied. She could barely speak as she was trying to catch her breath. There were scanty beads of sweat on her face.

Manvi followed him as he navigated her out.

"Thank God. Thank you, Mr . . . er . . ."

"I am Professor Abir Sharma. You can call me Abir," he said and offered his hand.

But before Manvi could reciprocate, he turned around as he heard a couple of people saying that the fire was small and had been extinguished.

Looking at Abir, Manvi asked him, "What happened?"

"I think everything is fine now," he clarified.

"Anyways, thanks, Mr Abir. That was so nice of you. I am Manvi Singh, a freelance journalist," she replied with a smile while extending her hand.

"So you are Manvi," shaking hands with her he repeated her name as if trying to recollect something. His big eyes got bigger as he exclaimed loudly, "Oh my God! You are Manvi Singh, the journalist?"

"Yes. But why are you so surprised?"

"Have you ever been to *Pandit* Anand Sharma?" Abir asked in the same tone, almost willing her to say yes.

"*Pandit* Anand Sharma, ummmm . . ." She took few seconds as if trying to remember.

"Oh yes! I have been there once with my mom. But how do you know?" Now it was her turn to be surprised.

Abir took a deep breath and said, "One more victim of *Rahu*." His cynical smile said it all.

"How do you know?" Manvi stopped again and looked at Abir as she wasn't able to contain her curiosity.

"I'll tell you. Actually, I had sent a very good friend of mine, Ashwin, to *Panditji* on the same day. He was there when you had visited him, the one who had given his turn to you," Abir replied.

"Yes I remember. So?" she asked

"So, *Panditji*, who is well known to me, happened to share this coincidence with me that God had similar plans for all three of us – you, Ashwin, and me."

"What plans?" Manvi was getting curious.

"If you could read the book of fate, it would be clear that we all are in the clutches of *Rahu*," he sounded serious this time.

"So what does Mr *Rahu* do to all three of us now?" Her ridicule was apparent.

Abir replied, "*Rahu*'s period will bring pains, sufferings, and struggle for us."

A giggle preceded a hearty laughter and with that, she shrugged her shoulders, twisted her lips, and thus presented her disbelief on platter. "Sorry to say but I don't believe in this *Rahu* thing. I am a journalist and I know hundreds of stories of pain, disaster, and suffering. You mean they all are afflicted by *Rahu*?"

Before Abir could respond, a loud honking distracted them. Manvi's car was blocking one of the exits.

Manvi, a little panicky now, ran towards her car saying, "Bye, see you, Mr Abir. Thanks for everything."

She jumped into her car and drove off, waving to Abir who had no reaction time. He smiled and waved back, disappointed that he had lost a great chance of knowing her whereabouts that Ashwin would have liked to know.

As Manvi reached her home in Sector 2 and walked into the family room, she saw Dr Uncle, her mother's cousin, sitting there. She wished him and plonked herself on the sofa.

"Are you all right?" Manvi's chain of thoughts was interrupted by Dr Uncle's concerned tone.

She replied with a little yawn, "I'm fine. It was an eventful day today."

She stretched herself and continued, "But very tiring. The conference couldn't come to its finish as there was a small fire".

"Fire!" Mom ran from kitchen, hearing the word 'fire'.

"Mom, it's okay. I am fine. It was a *small* fire." Manvi tried to put her worries to rest. "The conference I went to cover today, was addressed by Mr Samar Taneja, a young entrepreneur . . ."

"You mean Samar Taneja of Meditech International?" Dr Uncle didn't let her complete and asked.

"Do you know him?" Manvi asked.

"Oh yes! I know him. He is a thorough gentleman. An achiever in his own way," Dr Uncle replied. He seemed to be in absolute awe of Samar.

By that time Mom came back with a glass of water, and three cups of coffee.

"Who's he?" Mom quizzed.

Dr Uncle looked at Mom. Nodding his head, he picked up his coffee and said, "That's Samar! Hardly thirty and he has made a niche for himself."

"Not only that," he continued catering to her mother's inquisitive glance, "His magnanimity is well known as he donates generously and works for the underprivileged!"

'Samar had announced a huge charity for the treatment of cancer patients even that day', Manvi recollected.

"But one can't fight one's destiny. God hasn't blessed him with privilege of a happy married life," Uncle suddenly grew sombre.

"Why so?" Mom posed a short question, perhaps in a hurry to know the answer.

"His wife's parents are settled abroad and she was keen to go back to them permanently, but he didn't want to leave his ailing mother alone."

Manvi's mother asked with a tinge of interest, "But how do you know him?"

"Last year I operated upon his mother's knees. Oh! I wish I had a son like him. Truly, what a boy!" Dr Uncle carried on with praises of Samar.

Samar's innocent eyes, greenish stubble, and suave persona emerged as imagery at its best in Manvi's mind. Manvi excused herself and went to her room to escape that conversation.

A little later, she lay in her bed deliberating, "Mom would love me to fall for this gentleman, if he is one."

She shrugged her shoulder and muttered, "Where is love these days? Today's world is too busy to indulge in such a wasteful emotion."

She slowly slipped into a deep blissful sleep.

A month later, she happened to meet Samar at her dad's reunion party. The party was good. Beautiful saxophone instrumental filling up the pleasant breeze of October evening added on to the charm of lush green sprawling expanse of Forest Hill Officers Institute, at an hour's drive from Chandigarh towards Shimla.

As they arrived at the party, Dad and Mom disappeared as if dissolved somewhere in the crowd. She quietly settled down on a sofa in a corner. Just then a soft pat on her shoulder from behind roused her out of her solitude.

"Samar!" Her mouth was wide open. "I mean, Mr Samar," she corrected herself.

"Manvi, call me Samar," extending his hand, he whispered. After exchanging greetings, he informed her that he was a special invitee as he was associated with the hospitals, empanelled with army.

"Oh! That's great but how come you know my name?" Taken by surprise, Manvi questioned.

"You told me," Samar's eyes were mischievous and so was his smile.

"Me? When?" She was actually confused.

"I am Manvi, sir. I would like to ask you . . ." He imitated Manvi's voice the way she had asked him a question in the conference. She felt a little embarrassed as he clicked his fingers in front of her dazed eyes.

"Oh God! Some memory! It means you remember the names of all the reporters who were there that day?" Manvi giggled.

"No, You are Manvi, that's why." He was quite blunt in saying so.

Manvi kept quiet, not knowing what to say.

"How come you are here?" Samar shifted the course of conversation smartly.

"My dad retired from army two years back. It's the reunion party of his regiment," she replied.

"Oh! I didn't know that your dad had served in army," he remarked.

"How would you?" she asked with a twinkle in her eyes.

"Right. How would I? Fine, now I would like to know everything about you, so that I avoid such embarrassment the next time." His smile was as infectious as his voice. He was a smooth operator, she noticed.

Regaining her composure, Manvi said, "Nothing much. I'm working as a freelance journalist and as an occasional radio jockey."

While she was engrossed in oozing out the vital statistics of her life, he bent and lifted her *saree's* corner from the bed of the dewy grass to settle it on the arm of the cane sofa with such sophistry that her whole being could not resist admiring the chivalry in disguise of such elegant and innocent flirtation. He brought one corner of the *sari* closer to his face, looked into her eyes and asked, "Hugo . . .Hugo Deep Red?"

"Ummm . . . yes." She took time to react. His intrusion into her very personal space was so spontaneous and sudden. She was reminded of his audacity on the day she saw him first in the conference.

A little unnerved, Manvi popped out a silly question, though reluctantly, "You have come alone? I mean . . . Mrs Taneja?"

His intense smile adorned his face once again. Perhaps he could sense her nervousness.

"I am waiting for one," he spoke with a mock sigh and a smile.

"Waiting for one?" She repeated his words with a childlike ignorance.

"Yeah. Fortunately or unfortunately, she is not a part of my life anymore."

A smile returned to his face but this time it was not the familiar smile, but a little dispirited one.

"Manvi." Just then Mom called out her name as she came looking for her. Then the most predictable happened. The moment Manvi introduced them, their conversation went on in search of a wishful conclusion.

On their way back home, the only thing Manvi's mom talked about was Samar, Samar, and Samar. His charm and merit both seemed to have struck the *needy* mother.

***

Unknown to me, *Rahu*'s net had been cast. It was closing in on my Manvi. It would have been a fatal punch, but fortunately for me, Bhuj happened.

I had gone to visit my brother, Col Rohan, a few months back in Bhuj. That evening we went to the officer's mess for tombola.

The late dusky evening, filled with the tinkle of glasses and giggles of the ladies, daintily mellowed down into night in the cool breeze, perfumed with the heavenly musk. I enjoyed the intermingling of the people after my elaborate introduction session with Rohan's colleagues. A cute-looking spacious cottage on a small hillock surrounded by two-stepped lawns was what the officer's mess looked like. I marvelled at the facets of life where life and death, sorrow and smiles, labour and leisure, walk hand in hand in the highest of spirits.

"Gear yourself up for the picnic," Rohan reminded Niki when we were having a chat after we were back from the mess.

"Oh yes! Mandavi. We are all set." Her theatrical expression was worth a grin.

"You will find it very interesting," Rohan looked at me and said.

"What time?" Niki asked.

"Tomorrow we are getting together at the mess at four in the evening and will be leaving sharp at thirty minutes past four. Any other question?" he asked.

"No, sir." A salute followed a naughty smile from Niki as she started clearing the table.

"Evening?" I asked, as it was against the norms of picnic time.

Rohan smiled and explained, "You know, evenings here are very pleasant and tomorrow is a full-moon night. The glory of moonlit beach is worth watching."

Next evening, sharp at four, we were in the mess. Young officers got busy in coordinating the vehicles and picnic essentials. After mingling around, I settled down with a magazine in a garden chair, waiting for the 'Charge of the light brigade'.

Weather was pleasant and the breeze was soft. An absolutely apt day for picnic.

"Hi!" A very pleasant voice interrupted my reading.

I raised my face. Suddenly, everything came to a standstill.

Her dreamy eyes seemed more talkative than her lips, when she said, "Hi! Mr *Rahu*'s victim, how come you are here?" She seemed to have recognised me in the first go.

"Hi . . . Manvi. Right?" I asked as if in a trance.

"Right," she replied with a nod.

"It's such a surprise! What are you doing here?" I questioned.

"I am here to do the follow up of the massive development of Bhuj, that had lost a huge chunk of its ethnicity and heritage buildings to the earthquake of 2001," she informed me.

"Yes, Abir had told me about your tryst with journalism," I acknowledged.

"Abir? Oh yes! One more co-sufferer," she said and giggled.

"I believe you both met a couple of months back," I smiled and added, "where he philosophised and advocated *Rahu*."

"Oh! I see. He divulged it all to you," Manvi continued to smile.

At that moment, Niki arrived and looked curiously at Manvi.

"Niki, meet my friend Manvi. She is a journalist," I clarified.

"You're a journalist! How adventurous! You know, I always wanted to be one. But his brother came in my life and all my options were over. So now I'm a good-for-nothing housewife," Niki was quite spontaneous as she finished her statement with a hearty giggle.

Manvi took Niki's hand in hers and said, "You know, I also wanted to be a housewife and have fun in the cosy comfort of the four walls. But you know, destiny lands us up at the counters least expected." A shadow of gloom covered her face when she said so.

"Ashwin, let's move. You also, Manvi," Rohan shouted from a distance.

The wife in Niki gave a frowned smile to her husband and muttered to Manvi, "Everybody other than me knows you, Manvi."

Manvi, adorned with a very innocent smile, clarified, "Actually, I am here since last one week and Col. Rohan's regiment is providing administrative support to a couple of press people. I am one of them. That's how they know me."

"Oh, I see," Niki said. She seemed more relaxed now.

We walked up to the huge military vehicle. I marvelled at the conversion of the army seven tonner into a comfortable lounge, with mattresses and cushions arranged in such a fashion that it certainly bore a feel of picnic. The space was enough to accommodate all the grown ups. The kids, along with their games and screams, were loaded in the second vehicle.

A makeshift staircase was placed below the open tailboard to climb up to the vehicle. I climbed first and then extended my hand to Manvi to pull her up. I could feel a strong sense of excitement as I took her hand in mine. She looked a little embarrassed as she settled down by my side.

She was dressed in blue jeans and a white top. I silently admired her charming looks. As the sleeping giant, the seven tonner, suddenly lurched forward, she almost got pushed into my arms. Her mere touch once again sent my pulse racing.

Soon everybody was singing, producing wobbly notes, some musical and some non-musical, lending spirit to picnic.

A journey of an hour came to a halt at Mandavi, a small seashore township. We could see a couple of army tents on one side where the advance party had already set up a working mess.

We got down and moved towards the waves. The beach had a line-up of a few coconut trees, swinging in the moistened and lovelorn breeze. The load of life felt lighter.

Young officers pitched up a net and started playing beach volley ball, cheered up by the ladies. The senior ones got settled in the shallow waters with chilled beer bottles. Happy noise of giggles and laughters clothed the part of beach occupied by us.

Such an evening had come after ages. It rekindled fond desires. Manvi and I walked along the edges of the lacy waves which were approaching the shore at very regular intervals. Nothing seemed wrong with the world that day.

As the day slowly crept into the bosom of the sea and the waves increased their whispering in the ears of the breeze, we all shifted to the rooftop of the nearby palace where the dinner was arranged. The palace belonged to an erstwhile king, whose present generation was settled in Mumbai. The breathtaking view from the rooftop floored us. The lawns of the palace were dimly lit up. Sea breeze left the colonnade of coconut trees restless, on both sides of the road, stretching itself from the main gate to the porch. Music was floating in the air that subdued the boisterous laughter of the men and the chattering of ladies. I was standing in one corner of the roof and enjoying the breathtaking view of the beach and the palace, drenched in moonlight.

Some couples were swaying to the soft rhythms of guitar being played by a young officer. The environs were laden with heavy breath of dew and romance. Lights were dim. I gathered all my courage to ask Manvi for a dance. And soon we were together with my hand around her tender waist and hers on my shoulder.

"Heavenly!" I whispered as we swayed to the tune of music.

After a while I spoke softly in her ears, "I always used to think about you. Where are you? What is going on with you?"

She smiled. "You mean you were thinking of the agonies incurred by *Rahu* on me?"

"I didn't want to see you in pain. I don't know why," I clarified.

She closed her eyes. The feel of her presence in my arms made my senses numb. There was no desire to speak anymore but to feel her . . . just to feel her so close to me.

"If the clock stops," I wished. The clock didn't stop but the guitarist did as dinner was called.

The party was soon over. During the drive back, Manvi, like everybody else, slept through the journey. We reached home, and retired to our respective abodes for the night after bidding adieus. She was staying at the guestroom of the officer's mess.

The next morning, I woke up quite early. I smartened up myself to have a breath of fresh air. But alas! The meddlesome designs of destiny had brought a cruel culmination of a short and sweet rendezvous with the Cinderella of my life. I received a text message on my phone from Manvi, "Got to go."

My ego did not allow me to call her and ask for the reason of her sudden disappearance.

***

The noiseless wheel of time had been carrying on life swiftly. Samar was tapping all his resources to get close to Manvi.

It was the eve of *Karva Chauth,* an Indian festival. On this day, wives observe fast and pray for their husbands' long lives.

Manvi's mom was busy with the preparation for the fast. The festival brought to Manvi the memories of the fateful day of her wedding.

Dressed up in the traditional red attire of a bride, she had walked out of the boundaries of her parental bliss with a huge bag of hopes, wishes, desires, and dreams. Like any other bride, she was ushered in with rose petals and scented solutions at her new abode.

She distinctly remembered the knock on the door that night as she waited for Neel. There was a weakness in her knees and her heart thumped as she got up and opened the door. Quite unexpectedly, she saw a middle-aged lady standing there, instead of Neel.

The lady hushed her up before Manvi could find out who she was. She had brought a video CD along with her. As she played the CD, Manvi was filled with a palpable sense of devastation. Her lawfully wedded NRI husband already had a live-in relationship. Her world came crashing down. She had walked out at that instant, her soul badly scarred.

Seasons changed, but Manvi's destiny had a natural enmity with change.

Neel was not ready to sign divorce papers and their case lingered on. Her father had been exhausted by the drudgery of dealing in dust.

As she thought about that fateful night, her eyes sourced two saline droplets. The burden of her past didn't have time to disappear from her face as her mom rushed in hurriedly and saw her wet cheeks.

"Manvi," the choked voice and mellowed tone of Mom failed to disguise her emotions as she held Manvi in a motherly hug.

A sudden shift and pep marked her voice when she said, "Remember *Panditji!* He clearly indicated that it was all about your stars. You know it's not you but *Rahu* in the seventh house that has done this. He said, "Now, *Rahu* is occupying tenth house, so look forward to . . ."

"Mom, stop this nonsense," Manvi interrupted her.

"No, it's not nonsense," Mom said and the glint in her eyes furthered her conviction as she continued, "I can see

your good time has come. All the *upaays* have paid off."
Mom's zealous tone did not surprise Manvi.

Manvi kept quiet as her mother held her hand and said
softly, "Everything is going to be wonderful. By the way, we
have been invited by Samar's mom for *Karva Chauth puja*
tomorrow."

A reluctant Manvi accompanied her mother to Taneja
Mansion the next day. It was an imposing house and so
were the adornments for the *puja* ceremony in the sprawling
lawns. The surroundings were filled with the aroma of
flowers, sweets, and burning incense sticks. Samar's mom
was busy welcoming ladies in shimmering bridal costumes.

"Manvi, right?" Samar's mom asked as she walked in.

"*Ji*, Aunty," she said.

She hugged her warmly and said, "How sweet of you to
come. You are not fasting, *beta*?"

Her question seemed to have cropped up as Manvi was
still in her casuals, which did not go with the occasion at all.

She found the flooding affection of Samar's mom more
incongruous than her attire.

Puja was on. *Panditji* was chanting prayers. Although
Manvi wasn't a part of the whole affair, she was thoroughly
enjoying the fervour. Suddenly, her gaze was glued to a
figure emerging from the lobby that opened to the lawn.
It was Samar, personable and elegant as always, dressed in
crisp white traditional *dhoti kurta*, with a red *tikka* on his
forehead.

"Taking eyes off him could be an exercise in futility for
any mortal female," she thought and asked herself, "Am I
falling for him?"

After the ceremony was over, Samar's mom gifted
colourful *dupattas* to all the ladies. Samar whispered

something in his mom's ears and both of them walked up to Manvi's mom. Samar handed over a huge packet to her.

On their way back, her mom opened the packet in the car and exclaimed, "Manvi, look at these beautiful *dupattas!* Samar bought these especially for you from Jaipur."

She was not yet ready for Samar's gifts. Just to make her mom happy, Manvi took the box and put it in her cupboard.

What inhibited her? She had no clue, no reason, and no explanation.

Perhaps her past never allowed her to take these liberties or perhaps *Rahu* did not allow the regeneration of the emotion called love. Why couldn't Samar find a place in her heart despite all his qualities and eligibility, she wondered.

***

Before our meeting at the airport in Delhi on 17 April 2012, I had met Manvi a month back in Chandigarh. That was the day I had met Samar for the first time. It was *Holi*, the festival of colours.

I remember that the pleasant weather was intoxicated. Spring was in its bloom. Colours were smeared on the face of the environment and the floral visuals were treating the city beautiful.

Manvi's dad knocked at her bedroom door in the morning.

"Gotta go to club. Manvi, get up, baby. *Holi hai,*" he said in a jovial voice.

The club was bustling with activity. Beering and cheering was on. All friends and foes were on the same frequency, and the world looked a perfect place, as God would love it to be. Manvi was here today, just for a daughter's reason to make her dad feel that everything was well with the world. It was working as she could see. He looked happy.

Her thoughts came to a sudden halt as she saw Samar coming towards her. The glint in his eyes was highlighted today as the rest of the face was hidden behind the vibrant hues of the reds and greens. The Greek god had been transformed into a coloured demon.

"Happy *Holi*," he wished her and stepped forward to put colour on her. He poured a few ounces of *gulal* in her hair. Manvi also reciprocated by applying colour on his face. Samar made her sit down and excused himself for a minute to get a drink.

As Manvi looked around, she was surprised to see Abir heading her way with a big grin.

Abir then put a *tikka* on Manvi's face and wished her. "Happy *Holi*, Manvi."

"Same to you, Abir," Manvi replied excitingly and asked, "How come you are here?"

"Sabeeha, my fiancée, invited me. She will be joining us shortly. Her father is also posted here," Abir explained.

"Oh, that's great! I would love to meet her," Manvi smiled.

Abir settled down next to Manvi as he wasn't too familiar with the people around.

"How are you, Manvi?" Abir asked.

"I am okay," she replied.

"I want to share something with you," Abir said.

"What?" she asked.

"Do you remember Ashwin?" he questioned

"You had told me about him on the day of the conference. I met him at Bhuj. Are you talking about him?" Manvi asked a little enthusiastically.

He was a little surprised that Ashwin had not mentioned his meeting with Manvi to him.

Manvi didn't know why suddenly she had become oblivious of the surroundings. Her urge to know more about Ashwin was quite spontaneous but incomprehensible at the same time.

"Our *Rahu* co-partner. Isn't he?" Abir continued.

"Oh yes!" she replied. Her expression conveyed that she was somewhere happy to share even same kind of sorrow with him.

Abir informed her, "He is coming here today . . ." Before he could complete, he said, "The devil, here he comes."

"Hi, Abir," I embraced him and said, "Happy *Holi*!"

I was happy to see my friend but the view of the chair next to his, infused an inexplicable rush of emotions into my heart, mind, and body at the same time.

"Hi . . . Manvi," I greeted her.

"You took time to remember my name. Didn't you?" Manvi complained playfully.

I think I wasn't too good at the art of deception. My face mirrored my jitters.

"How can I forget you?" I said, shunning all my inhibitions, looking right into her dreamy eyes.

"But why should you remember me either?" A naughty smile crossed her lips. Before the conversation could proceed further, Samar appeared.

"Come on, Manvi, you are not sitting in your editor's office," Samar pronounced aloud from a distance, without taking note of my presence.

Manvi waved and her gesture indicated that she was not interested. I felt good. Abir, a true friend, could read that wide and clear and congratulated me through a cheeky smile.

"Don't you like colours?" She asked me in a familiar husky tone. I heard it clear but brought my ear close to her and looked at her questioningly.

"I said, don't you like colours? Not playing *Holi*!" She raised her volume.

I got up and grabbed a pinch of colour from the *thali* of colours and applied on her cheeks. It meant the world to me.

But before the celebrations could begin, *Rahu* struck. Samar barged in.

"Samar, this is Ashwin, my friend," Manvi introduced me to Samar.

"Hi. Nice to meet you." The pace of his words was quite fast and his haste made his courtesy look a little awkward to me.

"Hi," I replied. But before I could reach out for my next word, he grabbed her hand and pulled her into the sea of coloured crowd.

The infinite realm of pain was seizing my whole being. She was going away and I was rooted there, lost and unsought.

"Is it me, Ashwin, who's always been in company of valour and colour?" I asked myself.

"Where's Manvi?" Abir asked, as he came back with two glasses of beer and a boy following him with *thali* of *gulal* in his hand. I raised and pointed my finger towards the horizon of the crowd. Perhaps, he could feel the sacred hunger of my ambitious heart.

"She will come back. She has to. Enjoy your *bhang* and beer. Sabeeha will also be here shortly," Abir encouraged me as we binged on the liquids.

All of Abir's actions and words were an excuse to distract the mind of a disgusted child, which was me. Abir was the only soul who knew the depth of my numbness.

"She would have come back if she really cared," I thought and decided to leave.

In the parking, as I turned towards my car, Abir pointed towards a shiny black Mercedes parked next to my car and said, "It belongs to Samar. The one who pulled Manvi away."

I kept quiet.

He hugged me as if to reassure me that everything would be fine.

I took one look at Samar's car and drove off.

I reached Hotel Mount Hill View in Sector 10, where I was staying for the night.

He that is used to go forward and findeth a stop,
falleth out of his own favour and is not the thing he was.

While walking through the corridor of the hotel I was thinking of these words of Bacon. How ironical! Not only I understood the meaning of those words that day but had experienced them too. I always had been an achiever. Cheers and happiness had always ornamented my very being. Had my heydays been devoured upon by *Rahu*? These thoughts were making me uneasy.

I took a shower, changed, and dropped dead in my bed, a combination of beer and *bhang* overriding my thoughts of Manvi.

I slept for quite some time. I woke up in time for dinner. I picked up the phone and ordered my favourite dish, spicy chicken curry and rice. My mood shifted its ground.

I looked at the shimmering Kasauli lights from the window and my thoughts went back to the afternoon. I had not only lost my train of thoughts when I saw her, but I had also lost all coordination of my being. I took my eyes off the Kasauli lights and shifted my glance to my dimly lit room. She was there. She was right there. She was beautiful, a beauty which grew more seductive, the longer I looked. Our eyes met and a bright smile lit her face. Her smile touched a chord in my heart that had never been strummed before.

I slowly walked up to her to wish her Holi. She was aware of my smell – primal and raw, and she was aware of her palpable fear and excitement warring with each other as I touched her. She was aware of the shadow of my face on her body.

"Happy Holi!" My voice both unnerved her and catapulted her excitement. She barely managed to swallow past the baseball lump in her throat. Unable to reply, she heard her own heartbeat and bated breathing in the absence of sound that followed.

She stepped back to free herself from my warm hand.

For a long moment she didn't answer, just stared into my eyes. The touch had been enough to send a pulse of hot arousal, tiny electrical changes, rushing through her. We could actually feel the sparks of energy darting between our bodies. It was like a magnetic force making her want to draw closer and closer still, until I walked away.

"Damn you, you are beautiful," I muttered.

"Manvi, you are mine," I screamed.

My heart was jerking like a jackhammer as all my senses now pined for her. I wanted her so badly that my entire body ached.

I could feel her presence in the room. I could visualise her very clearly as she walked towards me wearing a bright red sari *tied very low down on her waist, with a short sleeveless blouse exposing her beautiful midriff. She was wearing jhanjhars in her ankles which tingled as she walked towards me, a kamarbandh round her waist, a sparkling pearl set in her neck and ears, and kajal in her eyes.*

"You are mine," I said as the light breeze of my breath ruffled her hair. My work-hardened hands gently stroked her face. The touch of her hands on my body felt like a sensuous massage.

"There is nothing that I wouldn't let you do to me," I whispered as my lips covered hers. Tears filled her eyes as I worshipped her. The tears made her feel needy and greedy.

My fingers inched further along the smoothness of her skin, deeper, lower as she gasped in anticipation. I kissed her neck, her hot spot, and my fingers untied the kamarbandh on her slender waist. She could barely suppress a gasp of awareness at the tingle of excitement that radiated through her body. I undressed her as if annoyed by the whole convention of wearing clothes. Underneath was Manvi. There she stood, totally bare and real. Breasts full and perky, flat stomach, hips and thighs curving softly.

Our auras mingled with each other before our physical bodies did. It was as if the karmic connection from the last birth had continued.

"I love you. God! I have never loved anyone the way I love you," I moaned.

We had now become aware of the supreme flow of the sacred life force itself – the sacred unity of love. The experience of subtle energies within our sensual embodiment lead to enhanced pleasure as well as increased spiritual awareness of the erotic and ecstatic consciousness that pervades one's human embodiment.

We were locked together completely in a sacred experience depicting oneness of a distant monk. We were elevated to higher spiritual plane. We had harmoniously balanced the male and female energies to create spiritual ecstasy and achieved moksha.

"We are one! Manvi, we are one," I moaned.

Manvi looked at me, smiled, and closed her eyes as if in prayer.

My eyes were wide open in the aircraft as everyone around me slept. Thankfully, the lights had been switched off, and I lay uncomfortably ensconced in my blanket. *Holi* episode had happened just a month back and now I had met Manvi in Mexico.

I was desperate to solve the riddles but had no clue where to begin from. The first riddle had pointed to look for solace in the past. "Maybe Abir, the man of metaphysics, could help me," I thought. Over all these intriguing thoughts, I slowly slithered into sleep in my cramped seat.

Perched high, light in the sky vast, looketh for solace in the past;
Eastern art from ancient time, renders me the key, that maketh self
prime.

Gypsy's Riddle one

Chapter 6

2012
Chandigarh

The Wake-up Call

A few days after returning to India, I sent a text to Abir from office, "Bar-in-car, this Saturday."

"Are you back from Mexico?" Abir asked in reply.

"Yes, I was back on Tuesday," I responded.

"I have found a beautiful spot on the backside of the lake. We will go there this time," replied Abir almost instantaneously.

"Do bring Kotkapura chicken," he wrote again.

Kotkapura chicken is a wonderful dish prepared by a famous eatery in a small town near Ludhiana. The chicken is stuffed with condiments and dry fruits, then wrapped in dough and is cooked in its own juices in a coal-fired *tandoor*.

We reached the lake at 8 p.m. on Saturday night.

"Yum!" Abir cried out as he gulped down the first morsel of the delicacy.

"Cheers." We clinked our Glenlivet-filled glasses.

As we sipped our drink, Abir asked rather mischievously, "So any escapades on this trip?"

"Nope." My point-blank reply must have been a big blow to his expectations.

"But I had a very unusual experience during my last visit to Catanduva in Brazil." I thought of catering to his aspirations as I postponed raking up the riddles' issue for some time.

"What?" questioned Abir, as a smile full of vicarious pleasures escaped his lips.

My narration began. "I had to make an unexpected stop in this town about three months back. Due to an ongoing exhibition, all the hotels were full. Then my taxi driver suggested that he could get me an assured room in a village motel on the outskirts of Catanduva. Left with no choice, I agreed."

"Surprisingly, the motel was secured like a fortress. There was an elaborate security interview at the gate before the castle-like doors opened and we drove in. There were beautiful small hut-shaped rooms all around the periphery. I walked into my room which had a round bed, pink paint on the walls, pink-and-white décor, and an eating table for two. It was a very cute-looking hut with nice clean washroom. Something totally new for me was a drum-shaped platform just above the dining area. I learnt later that this rotating platform was used by room service to place dishes from outside without causing any sort of disturbance to the guests," I continued to give a vivid description as Abir, in rapt attention, forgot even to sip his drink.

"As I stretched myself on the bed, I saw that the entire ceiling was covered with a round mirror glass laced with lights. I switched on the TV to catch some news but all channels were showing only X-rated movies of varying degrees," I went on speaking.

I could notice an excitement building up in the eyes of Abir as he listened to me. I raised my glass to have a sip and he conveniently came in the way and pushed the glass back by forcing it down with the index finger of his left hand.

I smiled and continued. "The refrigerator was stocked with all kinds of spirits and wines. The room had an excellent collection of glasses that would have given a French restaurant a run for its money. I fixed myself a glass of scotch as I settled on my bed. Suddenly, I could hear the drum rotating and I saw a plate full of starters I had ordered on my way to the room."

"As I munched on the excellent Brazilian appetizer, I felt rather amused by the way it was served to me. Since I did not understand any Portuguese, it was difficult for me to converse with the room service as I placed my order for the main course. I had fixed another drink and was strolling in the room when my eyes fell on a pack of gifts meant for enhancement of carnal pleasures. These were various kinds of exciting costumes, bikinis, sheer garments, furs, hunters, and whatnot," I kept speaking like a sincere narrator.

I paused again to take a sip and realised that he had not interrupted me even once which was so unlike him. With eyes wide open, one hand under his chin, elbow resting on the window, he was no less than a child listening to an interesting bedtime story.

"So, that was a whorehouse! Did you have fun?" he questioned with absolute curiosity.

"Not exactly. I discovered that this was a place away from town where you could bring your partner and live your fantasies," I smiled and continued, "One had to bring one's own partner."

"And who accompanied you there, my friend?" Abir asked with a naughty smile.

"Yes, I was not alone," I replied with an equally naughty smile.

"Lucky chap! Who was she?" He almost shook my shoulder as his inquisitiveness was overlooking the boundaries of patience.

"Manvi," I said in a very matter-of-fact manner.

"*Manvi . . . ?*" he asked, perplexed.

"Not in person but she was within me as a part of my own being."

"So nothing happened," Abir spoke rather dejectedly, reclining on the seat.

"Well, the motel guys were very confused that how come I was spending the night alone. It was a first for them," I replied, again with a smile and looked at the quiet waters of the lake.

It was a beautiful evening as we watched the stars shimmering in the lake. We had rolled down the glasses of our car and could feel the pulse of the approaching winter. The local FM channel was playing beautiful romantic numbers. I was immediately transported into the world of Manvi. I could no longer hold back.

"I actually met Manvi in Mexico," I said. From my tone Abir could make out that this time I was serious.

"Oh wow! That's great! Did you proceed any further?" He looked into my eyes, the alcohol effect making them look a little dreamy, and my words a little philosophical.

I gave him a general description of what had transpired in Mexico. The graphic contours on his face reflected his concern for me as I narrated details of my meeting with Manvi and Samar.

"He is very rich, extremely good-looking, and a smart chap," Abir made a face and blurted out as if all these qualities were rather negative than positive.

I nodded absent-mindedly.

"The bugger also has a swanky Mercedes Benz car to show off," he carried on.

I kept quiet. I actually did not have any answer.

"It is very hard for any girl to refute his charms. I mean he has everything, with plenty to spare, that any girl could ask for. It is very tough for Manvi not to fall for him, and I guess she likes him a lot," Abir said as he put his hand on my shoulder as a consoling gesture.

The time had come for me to let Abir know about my meeting with the mysterious gypsy lady and her riddles.

"Something very strange but very interesting happened there," my words had stirred his snooping again.

"You know I met a very interesting crystal ball seer in Tequila village," I continued.

All antennae of Abir were up to catch the signals as the conversation had meandered towards his field of expertise.

"What did she say?" he asked with a zip in his voice.

"After she saw some images in her crystal ball, she talked about four very strange and inexplicable couplets that were going to shape my life," I explained.

"What exactly?" he queried.

I opened my wallet and took out the folded parchment on which I had noted down the prophecies of the seer. I had been very busy since my return and had not been able to give much time to them.

"She had forecast everything in riddles which I found very captivating," I said, opening up the sheet.

"This sounds really exciting!" exclaimed Abir.

I switched on the reading light and read the first puzzle aloud.

Perched high, light in the sky vast; looketh for solace, in the past;

Eastern art from ancient time; renders me the key, that maketh self prime.

"That is quite a riddle. As far as I can comprehend, she is talking about some incident in the past which gave you a lot of solace," Abir spoke with all his wisdom.

"I guess so, but which incident?" I quipped.

"Some kind of an Eastern art you learnt in the past, maybe in your last birth," Abir continued with his share of inputs.

"She did mention that these are the clues which will help me tread on the path of self-discovery and actualisation," I added almost philosophically.

"This certainly means that she must have seen something good that your future holds for you," Abir replied cheerfully and then proceeded to make the next round of drinks.

I slowly raised my head to the left to look at the stars in the clear sky. There, far away on the hilltop, I could see the gleaming Kasauli Lights.

"Wait a minute. Oh yes!" I mumbled in absolute engrossment and excitement after a few seconds.

The mystery was unravelled within moments.

"Remember? During the first year of Engineering, we had hiked to Kasauli on its narrow trails and just short of the top, I had wandered into a temple where the famous *guru* Jetchi from Dharamshala was giving practice in meditation," I reminded Abir.

"Yes. So?"

"I had joined the group as I felt fascinated by his talk and he had made us look towards the lamp post on the top of the hill. Those words are echoing in my ears, Abir," I said and got lost in that memoir.

As I was sharing all this with Abir, I started repeating the practice given by Jetchi. I pressed my first two fingers hard with my thumb and fixed my gaze on the Kasauli lights. I felt sudden transformation going on within me and my energy levels zoomed up as I was sure I had solved the first puzzle. I reached a state of calmness within moments. I smiled.

Abir was looking at me curiously.

"What happened? What are you doing? What are you looking at in the darkness and why are you smiling?" he questioned.

"I think I have cracked the first riddle," I said softly, while I was still on my nostalgic spree.

"Tell me!" He almost half screamed in excitement.

I recounted him the story of my past and said, "I had found deep solace in learning meditation at that time. Perhaps, my destiny is guiding me to practice this art further."

Abir nodded in agreement but did not say anything. Perhaps, he believed that I was not cut out for the meditation kind of spiritual discipline.

He took a big sip, laughed and with all the mischief of the world in his eyes, he said, "*Bhai*, when you go for meditation, please pray that I get married to Sabeeha soon."

I knew that he wasn't too serious about the whole concept or perhaps he was too sure about my logic supreme attitude since ages. So, I changed my track and asked him, "What is stopping you from getting married?"

"*Panditji* has asked me to wait for four more years. My seventh house, which is the house of marriage, is badly affected by *Rahu*. If I marry earlier than this, it will not work," he spoke in a low decibel. Twinkle of mischief gave way to dolorous dimness in his eyes.

"Four years is a long time. Lots of things change in four years. I am sure, Sabeeha will wait but there could be all types of social pressures on her family and her," I tried to suggest and it was a serious suggestion.

Abir didn't reply. He desperately wanted to get married but his impressionable mind was deep into the quagmire of *Panditji's* admonitions, which were feeding like a parasite on his insecurities.

I turned my head to the left and focused on Kasauli lights once again to seek a solution, pressing my fingers like before.

A moment later, I smiled and looked into Abir's eyes and said, "We will get you married soon, Abir." Perhaps, he didn't want to dishearten me or perhaps, my confidence was too overpowering to be questioned, he didn't.

After a moment's silence, Abir spoke again, "Wh . . . what . . . What is the second riddle . . . ?"

I picked up the paper from the car's dashboard and before I could read it out, my audience had been devoured by the spirit. Abir slumped on me with a thud.

I strapped him to the seat, cleared the itsy-bitsy mess around and started back. I was staying at Abir's place that night. After making him comfortable in the bed, I made coffee for myself, went out, and sat down on the easy chair in the balcony. I read the second riddle in the light of my cell phone.

Apparition blueth on the back, like a boulder;
Changeth white, on his shoulder.

An atheist! A disbeliever! I could be named anything because I had never believed anything that my eyes couldn't see. I was always a man of the physical and not metaphysical. But that day things were not the same and there was a reason to it. I was forced to think, "How could the crystal ball reader enter my brain and decode my imagination of blue apparition being that of *Rahu*. How? How after all?" I was questioning and answering myself at the same time.

"How did the lady know about this? Extrasensory. Was it?" I questioned myself time and again.

The intrigue shrouding the second line of the second riddle was still boggling me down.

I struggled for almost an hour but was not able to decode anything further.

I went inside to get some water as I felt thirsty. My sight caught the picture of Sabeeha adorning the top of the refrigerator.

"You will soon be here," I promised her. I needed consolidation to live up to my promise.

To get my friend out of the clutches of *Rahu*, to understand the logic behind the predictions of *Pandit* Anand Sharma and to unfold the amazing commonality between the predictions of *Pandit* Sharma and the gypsy lady in Mexico, I needed research. I needed books. I needed time to study, and I needed my teacher to refresh my knowledge of Eastern art, taking a lead from the spirit of the first riddle of the gypsy lady. The metaphysical demanded revelation.

I was always the one who needed reason for everything, from the time my very being gained awareness. My dad was right when he had said, "You are like Kipling, who believed that 'There are six honest serving men – When, Why, What, How, Where, and Who'."

As it was, I was planning to take a break from work for a few days. But now I needed to take a break from the world and worldly, to seek pleasures of knowledge to achieve the smaller goals to accomplish the higher ambitions. So I decided to take four weeks' leave from the office and go to Dharamshala to meet the teacher I had met in Kasauli.

My journey to self-discovery had begun.

A period of self-discovery . . . questions are answers . . . and the search of perfect joys . . .

Guru speaks

Chapter 7

Lamp in the Cave

I set out on a journey with a dream to discover the right spirit of my faith and the belief of many like Abir.

The drive to Dharamshala was a very scenic one. Surrounded by dense coniferous forests, consisting mainly of stately Deodars, Dharamshala is a serene and picturesque hilly town in the upper reaches of Kangra Valley. The snowline, with numerous streams and cool healthy climate, makes the environs very desirable.

The backseat of my car was packed with a score of books, a few DVDs, and a laptop. I had booked a cottage at The Sojourns for four weeks.

The room was comfortable, snug, and homely. It had a coffee maker, a microwave, and a small refrigerator in one corner. On request, they had provided me with a writing table and a cosy chair. I piled up my books on the table and stuffed my luggage in the closet.

As I opened the window of my room, I was dumbstruck. It opened to the balcony from where the view was breathtaking as it overlooked the magnificent Dhauladhar Mountains. The calm was heavenly, with no space for human voices with the exception of the sound of a hilly song being played on the radio of the labourers plucking tea at the far end of the teagardens, lending an awesome view to my place.

I decided to walk down to get a feel of the town. As I was driving in, I had noticed a very quaint-looking tea shop near the entrance. The small shop turned out to be a gourmet shop, serving special herbal teas and mouth-watering desserts. The shop had two floors. Lower floor was well laid with a few pieces of wooden furniture that didn't choke the room whereas the top floor had only carpets with low seating and multihued Chinese lamps hanging in the corners in the name of furnishing. The floor was covered with a red dragon carpet as a spread. Bright and colourful satin cushions enhanced the humble yet charming aesthetic appeal of the place.

I ordered a blueberry cheesecake to go with the premium mountain flavour Oolong tea, a Kangra specialty, as Robin, the owner of the shop, informed me.

"Couldn't be better," I murmured to myself, savouring the sip of tea, but he heard me.

"Yes, our cakes actually sell like hot cakes," Robin said and smiled proudly, thinking that the appreciation was for the cake.

I reciprocated his smile. In fact, I was mesmerised by the serenity of the place. It was apt for entertaining the huge library that I had brought along.

Very soon, I was chatting with Robin. Dressed in all woollens, he was about fifty years of age and had a very healthy glow on his face.

"So what brings you here?" he asked me, rubbing his reddish and swollen, typically hilly hands.

"I have come to meet the famous *Guru* Jetchi," I replied.

"Oh, Jetchi! He is in Triund nowadays. This is a 5 km difficult trek through the jungle and is quite a climb." His reverence for Jetchi showed as he spoke.

"That is great! Will you help me with the road map of that place? I need to be there as early as possible. Is there a place to stay?" I shot a couple of questions to him in one go. I realised that in the hurry to come here, I hadn't planned my visit too well.

"Forest Rest House would provide you a room for Rs. 500 per night. You can also hire tents from there. But be careful, the electricity and water are rare commodities," he cautioned me adding a dash of humour.

"I have to study a lot. In fact, your tea shop is an excellent place to sit down and read. I really like the ambience. It's perfect to study the subject I am dealing in," I informed him about the second reason of my being there.

He gave me a probing look.

Sensing his inquisitiveness, I told him that I was doing research on a subject that affects the life of all of us.

He kept looking at me, waiting for me to elaborate.

"You know, Robin, people believe that our lives and destinies are controlled by stars and planets. I am trying to find the truth behind this belief, or perhaps *disbelief,* and to find out how true is this philosophy and cause-effect relationship," I raised my brow and gave an honest reply to his question that he intended to ask but didn't.

I don't know how much he understood but Robin, with his arms folded in front of him, nodded slowly. "It's interesting. Very interesting. My wishes are with you, sir. You are welcome to come here whenever you want. We do have Internet facilities, if you would like to use," he said politely that left me amazed at the reach of modernism in lives. I wished that it could reach the minds too. He excused himself as my order arrived, saying, "Enjoy your tea, sir!"

I was cosily enthroned in my cushioned seat, sipping the steamy hot beverage and enjoying the cool evening breeze sneaking into the room through the window, when my eyes fell on a big picture adorning the opposite wall. The picture was of a white dove sitting on the shoulder of a bearded man. The painter had actually highlighted the bird in the picture and captioned it as "Dove of Peace".

I watched the picture in amazement followed by excitement. The solution was staring me at my face.

"Good lord! I have solved the second riddle," I exclaimed to myself.

I had to figure out just one thing now, *how to convert my perceived enemy in blue into a friendly peace-loving white dove.* I remembered *Pandit* Anand Sharma's words, "If *Rahu* had been in your tenth house, it would have given you name and fame."

I muttered to myself, "How can *Rahu* be my friend? How? Think . . . think."

I ordered another cup of the refreshing and rejuvenating herbal tea and looked out of the window, towards the glimmering snowline which had become greyish blue as it was fading into cold darkness. In that direction was my next destination, Triund.

Before going back to the room, I got a detailed road map and the complete knowledge of the terrain from Robin and stuffed my backpack with essentials for the trek.

I had an early breakfast the next morning and started off around 6 a.m., with a vaulting ambition in my sight and a rucksack on my back. In less than an hour I reached Dharamkot, which had some nice-looking cafeterias. I surrendered to my temptation of a hot cup of tea.

A jungle trail started from there which led me to an old temple after an hour's brisk walk. The track, thereafter, got a bit tough with steep curves and tougher trails. I stopped for a while at the Best View Café to beat the cold and take a break for coffee. I had another two hours' walk ahead of me, as I started again.

As I reached the hilltop, the view of the luscious valley, snow-capped peaks, and small cottages of the township below was so delightsome that it took away all my fatigue. Cool breeze on my face felt very refreshing.

"Manvi would love this place," I whispered to myself.

I headed for the guest house about which Robin had told me. The manager, a middle-aged local man, was very helpful.

"You can get noodles and eggs with tea now," he informed me about his limited menu.

It seemed that he had multiple duties to perform there. He had now donned the role of a cook.

The long walk had built up a strong appetite in me. I cleared off the plate in no time. The noodles had never tasted better to me.

Undoubtedly, seclusion values company. The manager of the guest house quickly got talking to me. By now he knew about my ambitions enough and I knew about his burdensome but humble achievements as the guest house manager.

"Where can I find *Guru* Jetchi?" I asked the manager.

"He is teaching a small group of disciples in a cave, about half a kilometer along the trail," he informed me. I thanked him and left in search of my *guru* after taking directions from him.

After covering a steep and zigzag track for about twenty minutes, I reached the cave. I would have missed the narrow entrance as it was covered with green shrubs and creepers. The cave was located by a gushing stream where every piece of green seemed to be enjoying the air it was breathing. I walked into the mysterious yet enticing darkness. The air was surprisingly warm inside. At a little distance, I saw a light originating from a bonfire. Three people in maroon-coloured robes, were sitting by the fire with their eyes closed, as if meditating. On the other side I saw someone sitting on a raised platform, probably a flat rock, covered with a sheet.

"Jetchi!" I just whispered the name. I couldn't help being extremely delighted at the view.

He had not changed at all since I had seen him last in Kasauli. His calm, composed, and serene face had the same radiance. He was wearing a warm white robe tied at the waist. Was it the sound of my approaching footsteps or was it my approach that made him open his eyes, was beyond my guess.

He had a sorcerer's mystique and an angel's charm that enveloped me as I entered the vicinity of his aura. I remember I had experienced the same peace when I happened to see him at Kasauli in the meditation camp.

I went near him, bowed and narrated all about my first encounter with him at Kasauli, years back. He blessed me and asked me to sit down in front of him. I didn't feel as if I was meeting him after so long.

"What brings you here, my child?" he asked softly.

"I am here to discover myself," my words were attired in a childlike hesitation, as I felt I was talking too big.

He smiled and closed his eyes for a few moments. I thought he had gone into meditation. But he opened his eyes just after a few seconds and with that emerged a sound. "Ask, my child. What do you want to know?"

"Can I change my destiny?" I questioned.

"Yes," he said. The simplicity and the earnestness of his answer surprised me.

"Why only yours, you can change the destiny of many," he replied.

"Me? How do I?" I asked.

"You will get all the answers before you walk out of this place in three days' time," he replied.

I nodded, as I waited for his further instructions.

For the next three days, every hour was a miracle. The confidence in me had started brewing that I would not fail in my noble endeavour. The unfurled robes of apprehensions were ready to be torn off.

He kept silent most of the time. We would get up at 3 a.m., drink two glasses of lukewarm water, freshen up, and sit in meditation for three hours in the cave. This was followed by the golden hour in which we could talk and ask questions. We would go to the nearby village to get vegetables and things of daily needs. Food was cooked by the four of us. No cell phone, TV, drinks, or noise around. I was in a world which was so different, so pure, and so wishful.

I pitched the tent I had brought from the guest house near the cave, by the tents of the other three people. We were usually back from the cave by 6 p.m. The spectacle of watching the sunset in the mountains was a visual treat to an urbane me, whose office hours always extended beyond dusks.

On the first night, lying in my tent by a blazing fire, looking at the stars, I thought about the first prophecy by the Mexican soothsayer.

I thanked the old lady whose first riddle had guided me to this Eastern art of ancient time. My mind was certainly evolving from an unreasonable atheist to a reasoned self-believer. I had learnt the art of taming my thoughts, the most important ingredient of self-actualisation, or meditation, if we can call it that.

But still I was not able to figure out the second riddle completely. Not that I had started believing in *Rahu* but there were Abirs in this world too who needed help. So the challenge was to have answers.

Therefore on the second day, during the golden hour, I asked, "*Guruji*, how can one make a friend out of a perceived enemy? How can one make peace with an illusionary figure who is supposed to be destroying you?"

He smiled and exclaimed, "Enemy!"

"Yes, enemy," I repeated, thinking that probably he hadn't heard me.

"It's you who can do it. Nobody else can do it for you." His voice was calm.

"But how do I do it?" My tone was indicative that I was not at ease.

"I gave you this answer many years ago. But now is the time when you need to understand it for the well-being of the world as well as your own. I will make you learn to tread the path that leads you out of the battlefield as a winner. Once you practice this, you will discover your answer." The expressions on his face were profound.

That evening, I spent two hours with him, learning and practicing the way to use my mind to tap the energies of the universe. To my utter surprise, he seemed more of a man of science rather than a practitioner of spirituality.

"Awesome," was the only word I could think of, once I finished meditating. For the first time I had experienced the quietness of mind, the weakness of mind, and its unrealised power.

Sitting in my tent the second night, I began my riddle-solving session again. But it was of no use. I shifted my focus to the third riddle and read it in the torchlight.

Riches got wings, as he wanteth 'em,
Goddess of fortune hasteth from heaven.

As I read the word 'riches', suddenly an image appeared in front of my eyes. It was Samar's Mercedes car and his act of paying money to the gypsy lady *in front of Manvi*. Samar's money was hurting me. Now I wanted abundance for Manvi's sake. Now I knew everything was possible.

"Everything possible?" I questioned myself. "Oh yes! Everything." I repeated the words again.

"If I want, the goddess of riches would bless me," I told myself aloud as my eyes scanned the third riddle.

"Oh my God, I have solved it. Yes, I did it. That's what *Guru* Jetchi said, anything is possible." My excitement knew no bounds.

I went to sleep driving my dream car, a black Mercedes, with Manvi sitting by my side dressed in a white *churidaar*.

The next day, I expressed to *Guruji* that I was able to find some answers but I still had quite a few questions."

He closed his eyes for a moment and then replied, "Ask your ego. *Ask and you shall receive*, remember?"

I spoke to my ego that evening during meditation.

Me: *Do you like it up here?*
Ego: *I like this calm.*
Me: *Do you like the meditation I am doing?*
Ego: *Yes.*
Me: *Do you know I have been trying to solve this puzzle about converting apparition blueth, I mean Rahu into a friend?*
Ego: *I don't believe in Rahu's existence.*
Me: *Okay! I agree. I also believe that Rahu does not exist but there are many who believe so.*
Ego: *I don't like the way Panditji scared me.*
Me: *You believe in* astrology?
Ego: *I don't know but I didn't like the fear psychosis created by your panditji.*

Me: Precisely. We are strong and are fighting back. What about
    Abir? What about Manvi? What about many others who
    are in his clutches. But there must be good ones too.

Ego: (No reply).

Me: Why don't you say something?

Ego: Abir is too ardent a believer of astrology. How will we
     convince him to use his mind? How will we get him out
     of the pandit's clutches?

Me: Oh, it's simple. Now is the time that he needs to realize
    the power of faculties of mind, the way we have realized.
    But I want your help.

Ego: Only to help friends.

Me: And other such people?

Ego: Okay.

Me: Are you with me?

Ego: Yes.

I had my answer. My introspection had led me to solve
the second riddle.

I remembered the picture of the *dove of peace* on the wall
of Robin's tea shop and smiled. The devilish blue *Rahu* had
been transformed into friendly Elfy, a white little angel with
smoky wings, twinkling eyes sitting on my left shoulder,
ready to help me attain the bounties that life had to offer. I
had moved *Rahu* from *enemy's house to friend's house.*

Was it meditation? Was it Visualisation? Or was it
simply to know how to tell your mind to make a heaven
out of hell.

Whatever it was, it had worked.

I was very happy that evening as I lay on my stomach in
my tent with my eyes up, watching the beautiful night sky.
My ego jumped in.

Me: *Are you happy now?*
Ego: *Yes, my fear is gone. Elfy is our friend.*
Me: *That is wonderful. Together we will win.*
Ego: *I like Manvi. Pray she comes.*
Me: *(No reply).*
Ego: *Why are you quiet?*
Me: *Samar has lots of money. We need to create wealth.*
Ego: *You think she will go to Samar because of his money.*
Me: *I don't know but I want the riches for her. I want her to have the best. Will you help me?*
Ego: *(Quiet).*
Me: *Will you help me?*
Ego: *Yes, but remember, money is only partial happiness.*
Me: *(I nodded).*

I lay quietly for a while, thinking about Manvi. Then I took warm water from my flask and prepared a cup of tea. I took out the page and in the dim light of my torch, I read the last puzzle.

Rainbow to learneth, seek divine energy to teacheth, depreciate delusive fear falseth, tribe you must reacheth.

I sipped my tea and munched a muffin I had brought with me. My mind was on the puzzle. The last line was clear to me that I had this divine duty to reach out to the tribe of my fellow beings like Abir who perceived the astrologers to be their destiny designers. I had to find a way to remove the kind of fear psychosis created by some, *not all*. But how? I needed to research. I had to wait.

'The next day, the most amazing journey of my life would come to its end or perhaps it was going to begin!' I thought.

During the golden hour on the last day, *Guruji* said, "Now, you are ready for the world."

I nodded my head and said, "Yes."

"Learn to control your thoughts. Thoughts have frequency with which they communicate with universe and the universe responds to them," *Guruji* added softly.

"But how do we know that universe is responding?" My childlike query brought a smile to his face.

"Your soul will let you know about your accomplishment. Your feelings will tell. Negative thoughts would manifest in bad feeling and the good feeling would mean that the universe is in accord with your noble desires."

I was at peace now.

"Have your questions been answered, my son?" he asked finally.

I again nodded my head in affirmation. "Yes, master."

He blessed me one last time and closed his eyes. It was a signal for me to leave. I didn't know what it must be like in heaven but this place was bliss beyond compare. I felt like being there till eternity. But I had *jobs* to do.

All three of us packed our bags to leave for Dharamshala. I had to go back to the guest house to return the tent.

I was a bundle of energy as I trekked back to Dharamshala. We stopped at a café in Dharamkot to have our supper and I took an auto rickshaw from there to return to my cottage.

The next morning I woke up early, took a shower, picked up my mat, and came out in the balcony with keys of heaven in my hand. There was a chill in the pre-dawn air. The skies were partially cloudy. I could see a couple of early walkers some distance away. I arranged my mat and sat down in *Padmasana*, facing east.

I opened my eyes three hours later. It had dawned on the hills. The darkness was releasing sunshine slowly. The birds were chirping, and the greens were swaying fresh in the cool morning breeze. The view was just awesome. My body felt light and the mind enriched. I smiled and thanked the universe before I thanked *Guru* Jetchi.

Back in the room after breakfast, I spent good two hours checking emails and relaying instructions to my colleague Jeetu, in the office.

Then I walked up to the tea shop with my laptop.

"You look ravishing!" the ever-smiling Robin accosted me.

"Gee, thanks," I blushed.

"So how was your stay with *Guru* Jetchi," he asked.

"Life-changing," I confessed and sat by the window, taking support of a scarlet silk cushion. The mix of the cool breeze and warm sun was a heavenly cocktail. I began my search of the missing teaser on the Internet. I took out the paper and read the mysterious words again.

Rainbow to learneth, seek divine object to teacheth,
depreciate delusive fear falseth, tribe you must reacheth.

I had learnt that the puzzle was hinting at the use of some divine object required to learn something about the rainbow.

Rainbow signified the seven colours. 'Seven colours, spectrum, wavelength . . .' I was trying to get a lead. After an hour of stumping search, I thought of looking for something which could measure frequency or wavelength of the seven colours.

I researched again with a new vigour. I was smiling half an hour later as I placed my order with a company down south for a frequency-measuring instrument. I had got what I wanted. I thanked the universe and the little angel sitting on my left shoulder, my Elfy.

I was back to my room after having a delicious lunch at a nearby Punjabi *dhaba*. I picked up one book from the pack that I had brought with me. I was bound to give back in full to every descending sun for the next twenty days for my skills to enhance. It was the start of a journey of a different kind for me.

The rest of my days in the hilly town followed more or less a similar pattern. I meditated, read, researched, experimented, and then read more to silence my doubts. I wanted to help people to learn to speak to the universe and convert their blues into whites.

I drove back on the twenty-eighth day with a song on my lips and a little angel on my shoulder. I was ready for the challenge. I had a plan for Abir, I had a plan for *Panditji*, and I had a plan for me, but I did not have a plan for Manvi.

In fact, my mind had one but my heart said 'no'.

Impact of Jupiter transition . . . learner and imparter of knowledge . . . bringing changes . . .

Astro speaks

Chapter 8

Lights of Kasauli

"Do you want to marry Sabeeha by this Christmas?" I sent a text to Abir on a late Friday night, a week after I returned from Dharamshala.

"Yes, but what a question, man! Why did you ask this?" Abir shouted with excitement as he called me immediately after he received my message.

"I will tell you. Meet me tomorrow at Willow Café at six in the evening," I replied and disconnected the phone.

He called back again. "Come on, *yaar*, tell me something, and where have you been for so long? No calls. Nothing. Just a few text messages that you were fine. Where were you?"

"I was on the lookout for life for you guys. Actually, I have been doing research on how to get you married to Sabeeha," I tittered.

As I was in a rush to send off a few mails to my Columbian customers, where the offices were finishing off for the week, I hurriedly continued, "I have to send a few important mails now. I will explain to you tomorrow."

But Abir was adamant to know, so he asked, "Tell me what kind of research are you talking about?"

"Well, it was a research on the gypsy's riddles," I replied half smilingly.

"At least text me the riddles. Let me try to solve them in the meantime," he requested.

"Okay, see you tomorrow," I said and hung the phone.

I sent the riddles to keep him entertained for the night. I had also requested Manvi to join us the next day.

Abir was the first one to reach Sector 10 market the next evening. He was pacing up and down in front of the café when he noticed Manvi driving in. He was all chivalry as he opened her door and greeted her.

"Hi Abir," she greeted him back.

She got out of the car, looked around, and asked, "Where's Ashwin?"

Abir looked at his watch and said, "He will be here any moment."

The winters were setting in and it had started getting cold. It was good to get into the cosy comfort of the coffee shop. Abir placed the order for coffee, and they moved towards our favourite corner.

As they sat down, Abir remarked, "Ashwin told me that you had a great time in Mexico."

"Well, yes. We had a great trip," replied Manvi, but she made a hasty enquiry, "Ashwin told me that there is some important discussion coming up today. Any idea?"

Abir replied, "Apparently, you all had met a gypsy lady in Mexico who had prophesized an excellent future for Ashwin if he could solve a set of riddles. He has been working on them ever since he came back and . . ."

"He never mentioned about any riddles or any such thing to us," Manvi expressed her ignorance and continued, "But what magic is he going to do to help you?" She smiled and teased Abir.

"I mean he has figured out a way so that I would get married by this Christmas," Abir responded a little shyly.

"It's great news.Congratulations!" She patted his shoulder.

"I am not too sure," Abir replied with a glum face and carried on, "Let me see what solution Ashwin has. But it's a strict no from *Panditji*."

"I am sure things will work." Manvi tried to cheer him up.

After a moment's silence, she asked, "What are the riddles you were talking about?"

Abir was quite excited as he pulled out his phone and read out the riddles.

"What do they mean?" Manvi asked.

"I have been able to decipher some parts only. I believe Ashwin has been working on them . . . Oh, here he comes." Abir had seen me approaching.

Abir hugged me and Manvi complimented me with a smile, "You are looking very fresh, Ashwin!"

"Gee, thanks," I relished the appreciation.

Abir looked probingly at the sheets in my hand. I waited for the coffee to be served before I handed over a blank sheet to Abir and said, "My friend, this is a serious job. It's time to launch the offence to unhouse your liberty. Please write your goal, keeping your wedding in mind."

He looked curiously at me. Perhaps he was expecting something more magical. He took the paper and wrote, "I want to get married to Sabeeha."

Manvi, thinking that she also had been shoved into the war, looked at me and took another sheet, like a soldier with 'not to question why' attitude, oblivious to the fact that the orders were not for her.

I smiled at my innocent follower in Manvi, but shifted my attention to the target again. I looked at what he had written and took on a more serious avatar. I knew I was going to need a lot of coffee that evening. I had a long sip, cleared my throat, and started my monologue, "Look, you need to understand some basic concepts of goal-writing and its realisation."

They both nodded as I continued, "It is a commonplace knowledge that everything in the universe is some form of energy, vibrating at some frequency. Your coffee cup, this table, your thoughts, even you, me, and Manvi, all vibrate at different levels and at different frequencies." I smiled, looking at her.

Abir tapped at her hand and chuckled. "Are you vibrating?"

"Silly," she replied, making a cute face, and I could see that the formality was completely impaired as they both were bound by a commonality of going through a unique experience.

I continued, "One thing more, whatever we see is not an actual reality. We are just bundles of energy and we vibrate and attract situations according to our dominating frequency."

"I didn't get that," Manvi said.

I clarified, "Well, what you see and what happens to you is the result of your own perception. We are just like radio-tuners. From this vast storehouse of energy called universe, we pick up the frequencies falling within the range to which we are tuned."

Abir shifted in his chair, leaned forward, and asked, "If this is so, then where is the control of this frequency and how do we measure it?"

I got up, stood behind Abir, placed my hands on his shoulders, and said, "Good engineering mind, Abir. Wait for some time till we come to the measurement part. Today, let me focus on the control mechanism. Okay?"

I continued, as he nodded, "Your thoughts dictate your destiny. You magnetise those situations which are in resonance with the frequency of the thought you have let out in the universe. Soon those situations will manifest in your life and shape it up accordingly."

"Here's the clue. Riddle number four. Remember?" My grin clearly indicated that I was excited. Abir opened it on his phone. Without giving any reaction time to Abir, Manvi almost pounced on the phone to see the riddle. I took out my own phone so that I could read it to them.

As I was busy looking for the riddles, Manvi held her sheet with both her hands, raised it to screen her face, and whispered to Abir, "Does it make any sense to you?"

"Not exactly," Abir also raised his sheet to cover his face and said softly, twisting his lips like a dullard.

"Let's get serious. It's a question of my marriage, Manvi," Abir whispered again.

"Oh yes," she smiled and they both brought their sheets down.

I was back in the PEC auditorium giving a lifetime performance, my hands rising and falling like that of a magician as I summed up on a higher decibel, "You ask and the universe delivers!"

Abir looked at me quietly for a minute and asked, "In that case, how do I control my thoughts?"

I came close to him and said, "A negative thought will invariably manifest into a bad feeling. That's your body's feedback mechanism, which you need to supervise. If you are feeling bad, change your thought to a positive one and you will immediately feel good. Thousands of thoughts pass through our mind in a day, but only one at a given time. And that is the best part of human mind. The idea is to maximise positive thoughts. Get that?"

Abir was looking less confused now, as he asked, "But the point is, how does all this help me to marry Sabeeha?"

"Go and propose. What's the big deal?" Manvi shrugged her shoulders and suggested.

I smiled just to tickle Abir and said, "The girl is ready in his case, but not his *Panditji*."

"Is it funny?" Abir retaliated.

I smiled again, picked up the sheet from the table, handed it to Abir, and said, "Now let's proceed further. I want you to write your goal statement in the present tense. If you write in future tense, the universe will listen to your thoughts and will keep postponing it to future, understand? Now write as if you have already achieved the goal. For example, write, 'I am getting married to Sabeeha' instead of 'I want to marry Sabeeha.'"

Abir nodded again as I got up from my chair and stood up tall, smiled, winked at him, and added, "Since you are creating reality, it would be good if you could add more details involving all your senses such as how beautiful she is looking, where is the wedding being held, what time is it, aroma of the food being served, how are you feeling now. Pen it all down, my friend."

The looks on Professor Abir's face suggested that he was ready to write his Thermodynamics paper. He had always been wonderful in that subject and could take that paper even in his sleep. Seeing the same confidence on his face, as he pounced on the sheet, brought me an immense sense of relief. I knew, the value of this part was very intrinsic to the success of our mission.

I called for Jack, ordered coffee again and also Manvi's favourite, brownies with hot chocolate sauce.

"Congratulations, my friend. Let us celebrate your wedding." I passed on the brownies to them.

"Well, December 23 sounds good. It is holiday season and more than that it's my lucky number. Moreover . . .er . . .

I think it's a Sunday. No?" Abir asked Manvi excitingly, after counting on fingers.

I felt like an examiner who wanted to pull the sheet out of a student's hand because his time was up. My purpose was different though.

"Firstly, I don't want a detailed essay on your wedding itinerary, my dear. Secondly, I don't want you to get into your post-wedding state, that is your honeymoon," I chuckled.

I shrugged my shoulders and teased him, "See, I have nothing against it, but don't you think it would be a little awkward in the coffee shop."

Actually I wanted the whole procedure to be short and crisp enough to be practiced everyday.

I folded his sheet and put it in an envelope, gave it back to him and said, "You will live your dream at least twice a day till you achieve it. Okay?"

Abir again nodded his head. I knew he still had many questions. He was always the kind who asked plenty of questions in the classroom. Sometimes they were too irrelevant, but sometimes they had a very important agenda which was to draw attention.

"But *Panditji* will never agree for wedding in December this year," he made a statement which was more of a question.

If this had been a drawing class of Professor Aggarwal, Abir would have probably got a couple of scales on his knuckles, but this being the class of the life-coach Ashwin, the approach had to be more human.

I spoke calmly, "Abir, get this negative thought out of your mind by speaking the word *cancel*, twice. I assure you that *Panditji* will agree. Please set up my meeting with him tomorrow. Switch over to your wedding thoughts please. *Now!*"

My emphatic 'now' helped.

Manvi also started scribbling, though I had my instructions only for Abir. But my concentration wasn't enough to save myself from the innocent pleasure of watching her follow me blindly. So I let her.

Within moments, smile returned to Abir's face.

"See, it works," I quipped.

I analysed that his mood was now on the upswing and that I could feed more technical jargons into his open mind. You could call me a manipulator, but I had a job to do. Timing is very important in such cases.

Manvi's involvement clearly indicated that she had established a bond with the concept. Absolutely engrossed, she said, "Abir, here I agree with Ashwin. All our scriptures, *gurus,* and philosophers hold on to this view that if your mind can conceive and believe in a solution, you can achieve it."

I added on, "Yes, you are right, but one has to work on it. You see, the universe is the source of infinite energy. You have to tap the energy in a well-planned way, using concepts developed by theories of mathematics and constructive physics to achieve your goals. Okay?"

Perhaps it was heavy on Abir and even heavier on Manvi. Abir gave me a confused look again. "Physics and mathematics' usage to achieve my goals! How? This doesn't gel."

"A double 'how', Professor Ashwin." Manvi was a little louder than usual.

I explained, "Even physics theories are nothing more than succinct mathematical approximations of reality. These approximations are further limited by theory's basic assumptions, stated or unstated. Fine?"

A big 'yes' came from Manvi as if she could get into the depth of these complexities. That made both Abir and me smile.

Abir nodded his head, as I continued, "Even Newton's Third law has a fundamental assumption that action and reaction is simultaneous, which is not true. This profound restriction on Newton's law brings time into equation, which leads to the concept of connective physics. This addition of time-delay is physically significant in any system where there is a sudden or abrupt action or where the system by its size or nature is slow to react."

"Wait, wait. I am boggled. Now, I can't handle this one, Ashwin." Manvi was loud again.

"Even I don't understand how this theory of time-delay would help my marriage take place when I want. What are you leading to?" Abir questioned in astonishment.

"My friend, unlimited energy of the universe can be tapped, provided the way of extracting it precludes having to pay the price of reacting forces," I replied.

Abir didn't speak for a while as he collected his thoughts to question me. Finally he asked, "How can unlimited energy be harnessed? Do you have any scientific backing?"

I pointed to the sheets in the envelope and said, "I have explained the concept of infinite energy response from the universe by using time-delay application."

Manvi fiddled with the sheets and asked me in almost a hapless tone, "Can you give us a simple example?"

I proceeded on with a layman approach and asked Abir, "Do you remember Mr Kumar, the karate expert in Sector 11, YMCA?"

"Everybody from our batch knew about him. He was mad after Nandini from Electrical. Well, what about him?" asked Abir in a matter-of-fact manner.

"Do you remember, he used to break a concrete block with his unprotected fist. How do you think he was doing it?" I asked.

Abir opened his mouth and then shut it. He had this habit of doing it when he had no answers.

I demonstrated the reply, "The use of sudden force which is very quickly retarded is an essential element of karate. Effectively, the karate hit enters the system, does the damage, and then exits before the system can fully react and impart a reaction upon his fist. It not only increases the power of the hit but also saves the fist from whatever retribution the struck object might inflict via an action-reaction scenario."

Abir understood this well. He got so excited that he got up from his chair and yelled, "Yes. I understand now. Even Bruce Lee used to send his opponents flying ten feet with the movement of his fists, moving only one or two inches towards the opponent and quickly retracting in order to avoid the backlash of the action." Abir was clearly in the Archimedes mode now.

"Oh! Now I get it. It's all the whirligig of time. 'Time passes, time the consoler, time the anodyne'," Manvi sighed and uttered this literary jargon.

It was our turn this time to raise our brows as a reaction to this philosophical outburst which we couldn't comprehend.

"What?" The sound of two men of science in unison generated a pleasant smile on Manvi's lips.

"Nothing," she said and made a gesture with her hand as if saying 'carry on'.

I just grinned.

Abir's cliché was there once again. "*But* how is all this going to help me to marry Sabeeha on December 23?" The extraordinary stress on 'but' and the plight of the poor chap made us burst into a hearty laugh.

I knew the time to pass on the secret had come.

Notwithstanding 'his couple of notches lower' enthusiasm, I cleared my throat and spoke, "I am going to pass on a technique to you. The details are in this envelope. You have to practice it twice a day and Sabeeha will be yours."

I passed one envelope each to both of them. Abir was keen to open but checked himself as I told him, "Let's pay the bill and walk down to the leisure valley where we will practice this technique."

I could see Manvi fiddling with her sheet as I was paying the bill.

Abir, clutching on to the information sheet like a lifeboat, said, "Come on, let's move."

Abir's haste was a welcome move as he was a wilful man now. It was a little cold out there but Abir was oblivious of it. I saw Manvi wrapping herself in her arms while walking on the cemented pathway in the Leisure Valley Park. I offered my jacket to her. She took it after some initial reluctance.

I made them sit on the bench and asked him, "Abir, are you ready? I am going to teach you Kasauli Lights Technique or if you want, call it KLT."

My comforting conviction that Manvi would be eager too, brought a smile to my face as I asked her, "Would you like to practice?"

"Yes, I would. I'm sure it would be of great interest to my journalistic instincts," she replied and carried on, "But before we proceed further, please tell us if you have found out what do the riddles mean?"

I took a deep breath and replied, "Yes, I have."

"Oh wow!" she interjected.

"But first you need to understand certain things. All is mind. Our universe is nothing but a floating, giant, intelligent, invisible field of energy with infinite potential. We are in connection with this field through our mind by using its natural faculties."

"What natural faculties?" Abir questioned.

"Mind has the power of meditation, transformation, manifestation and reasoning, which are its natural faculties. All the riddles of the old gypsy lady are correlated to these," I replied.

"That's great, but what is the correlation," Manvi asked, a little perplexed.

"Let us understand the Kasauli Lights Technique, and you will have all your answers," I replied.

Abir, a little tense due to the fear of the unknown, looked at me and said, "Let us get started then."

"Look up forty-five degrees, at twelve o'clock," I started.

Abir and Manvi both looked here and there confusingly. Abir finally settled to look up in front over the trees towards the hills. Manvi looked at her watch and then followed Abir like a lamb.

I carried on, "Now, see how the galaxy of Kasauli lights, with radiance of glory, offers a bliss beyond compare. See them. Drown yourself in them. Let your sense of sight override your sense of touch. Feel the softness of the cloud of brightness, caressing you as you pass through the galaxy." My voice was soft and soothing.

I could see the soft smiles and the traces of serenity on their faces that assured me that they followed correctly. I went on, "On the other side of Kasauli lights, see the furry trees, dark-green with slender tops, and snow-clad peaks and those small beautiful cottages by the side of the gushing stream. The nature has let loose its splendour."

They both did as instructed.

I was trying to slow down their frequency both physically and mentally.

Abir had a quiet expression on his face as I continued, "You are now standing in front of a big white hillside covered with snow which serves as your canvas. Paint your picture on this canvas. You see a new successful you getting married on December 23 to Sabeeha."

"Yes, I can see that happening," Abir spoke with a blissful smile.

"What do you see, Abir?" I asked in a soft voice.

"We are in Kasauli Club. It's my wedding day," he replied.

"Who else do you see?" I asked gently.

"I see Sabeeha, my parents, you, and lots of people," he answered.

I was tempted to ask him if he saw Manvi there with me but I exercised control.

"Any aromas there?" I continued asking.

"Ummmm! Aroma . . . *Hyderabadi Biryani.* It's so good," Abir licked his lips as he replied.

"Is there any music?" I questioned.

"Yes, the whole place is swelled and sweetened by the melodious humming of *shehnai*," he affirmed.

"Now you are feeling the texture of the long red silk scarf whose other end is in Sabeeha's hand as you are now taking the wedding wows," I said.

"Yes, yes . . . oh yes," Abir's elation was more than evident.

"You are in your alternate universe now, Abir. You have to resonate at the frequency of the successful you, the one you are creating, Okay?" I asked.

"Yes," he replied.

"I will tell you now how to do it. *Do you see an energy cable in the hands of the successful you?*" I asked.

Abir nodded and I carried on further, "Hold the other end of the cable and squeeze. As you squeeze, you will notice a controlled white energy flowing from the cable to you. It will help you to receive energy from the successful you and will try to match your dominant frequency with that of the successful you," I explained.

"Wow! I can actually feel the flow," exclaimed Abir after a while.

"Do this for a minute. You can control the energy flow by the squeeze on *energy cable*," I suggested.

"All right," replied Abir.

I left Abir alone for a minute and looked at Manvi. I had no clue about the subject of her thoughts.

Manvi had a solemn stillness on her face. Today again, she was dressed in my favourite white *churidaar* suit. My jacket was keeping her comfortably warm. I could sit here watching her for hours and hours.

"Now, count till five and slowly open your eyes," I told Abir.

He slowly opened his eyes. He was looking fresher and happier.

"Always show gratitude to the divine energy of the universe that brings you everything you want," I concluded.

Abir gave me a big hug and said, "I understand that *energy cable* is a source of transfer of universal energy from the successful virtual reality to me. Correct?"

I put my arm around him and nodded.

Manvi opened her eyes slowly and smiled at me.

"What did you see, Manvi?" Abir asked her. He knew that I would be curious to know.

She replied as her philosophical self resurfaced, "I saw my past, present, and future abiding by me."

"That's great. That's the spirit of the whole concept," I gushed at her receptivity and carried on, "But I am still amazed by the correlation between the old gypsy's riddles, Kasauli Lights Technique, and the connectivity to the universe through the human mind. In fact, I am stunned!"

Before I could elaborate further, Manvi asked in a mischievous tone, "Ashwin, I was also there the day you met the crystal ball reader. How come you never told us anything?"

"You were too busy," I said, not denying that my words were laced with sarcasm.

"Busy? Where?" she asked so innocently that I dismissed all my sarcastic stint.

Abir, who was still stuck at the point I was trying to make, looked at me and asked, "Tell me about this correlation thing."

I replied, "See, the first riddle points at the fact that the *power of meditation* is a very strong faculty of mind which allows us to live as the watcher and the doer simultaneously, just as you did when you watched your mind's movie play. This enables us to instantly access the moment of awareness where we free our mind of limited conditioning. Didn't you notice that when your mind became free of the conditioning done by *Panditji*, you were able to see your goal being fulfilled."

"Oh yes! You are absolutely right." Abir nodded in agreement.

I continued, "The second riddle talks about the transformation from the eerie blue apparition to the white dove of peace. The *power of transformation* is the second faculty of mind which can convert lower and negative emotions into higher and positive ones."

Manvi added, "You mean, think right and achieve the desirable?"

I replied, "*Perfecto*. See, Manvi, even you can also transform your fears into blissful happiness."

"Amen!" Manvi was looking at me constantly as I was talking and I liked it.

"Wow! That gypsy lady was something," Abir interjected and asked, "And the third riddle?"

I continued, "Yes, she was. See the third riddle talked about creating abundance and how would I do that? Obviously by using another very strong faculty of mind, the *power of manifestation*. We attract what vibrates at the frequency of the vibration of what we emanate out into the world. One needs to consciously generate resonance that matches with the frequency of abundance." *The human that I am, Samar's riches floated in my eyes.*

"You mean I can also grow rich by using this?" Abir asked excitingly.

"Yes, you can. But right now think of enriching yourself with an asset called Sabeeha. No?" I replied winking and smiling at him.

Abir's enthusiasm knew no bounds by now.

There was a moment of silence before I carried on, "Quantum physicists say we live in an observer-created reality. You know the strongest faculty of mind is the *power of observation*. We create what we bring to our observations."

Manvi said, "I believe you are talking about 'visualisation'. You mean visualise what you want to achieve and it will be yours."

I knew Manvi was on the right grid as she said that.

"You are not as dumb as you look, Manvi." Abir didn't miss the chance to pull her leg. She boxed his tummy softly and smiled.

Abir kept quiet for a moment and then asked, "Do you mean to say that I have delayed my own wedding by making the delay a reality, by believing in *Panditji*?"

"Absolutely," I replied, "We choose our possibilities with our intent."

"I have to visualise myself getting married on December 23 this year rather than to live in the fear of failure. I just hope that these two situations do not coexist," Abir expressed his concern.

I replied, "I will ensure that *Panditji* stops talking about failure or the delay of your marriage. At the same time, I want you to understand that the *power of uni-thought* is another strong faculty of mind which you need to practice. It gives you the power to focus on one thought at a time."

"So, Sabeeha, Sabeeha, and Sabeeha and no other thought. Okay, Professor Abir?" Manvi giggled as she teased Abir.

Abir gave a shy smile and nodded.

I held Abir's hand and said, "When you master your mind, you master your life."

As we reached my car, Abir said, "I feel more confident now. Let us get a nod from *Panditji* tomorrow."

Apparently, Abir was still nursing a fear of failure and he was not fully employing mind's power of transformation.

"Please fix up my meeting with *Panditji* and I will convince him. Okay?" I assured.

"Yes," he said.

Suddenly, Manvi chirruped, "Hey, guys, I have a wonderful idea!"

We both did not speak but gave her a quizzical look.

"Are you okay with a chat show on radio?" her eyes widened with excitement.

"Chat show?" I asked.

"Yes, chat show. I think it's a divine right of the people in distress or dilemma. Such a wonderful concept needs to reach the needy ones who are suffering at the hands of fortune-tellers, I mean the unscrupulous ones. No?" she asked and softly added, "Only then your fourth riddle will get manifested."

I was amazed with her input. She had been able to solve the fourth riddle to quite an extent.

"But what does the fourth riddle mean?" queried Abir.

I smiled and said, "Think, Abir. You will come to know about it in the near future when we meet *Panditji*. It is all about mind's power to reason when you have to make a choice."

"But why do you want *Panditji* for this?" Abir asked.

"Why not? *Panditji* would talk about the destinies written and Ashwin would talk about the destinies made," Manvi said and added, "Besides, the chat show would bring tremendous publicity to him. Why wouldn't he?"

I was in absolute agreement with Manvi as I said, "Now it's your job to get his consent."

Abir finally saw some wisdom in our words and promised, "Done. Getting him to the chat show is my responsibility."

I was happy at my achievement. I slept merrily with my jacket in my arms.

Abir visualised both his wedding and post-wedding ceremonies, as he told me the next day.

Manvi had a blissful smile on her face as she lay on her bed, thinking about Ashwin's words, "See, Manvi, you can transform your fears into blissful happiness." Perhaps, she was on her way to shed her baggage of the past.

Just then her phone rang. Her smile got wider. It was Samar calling.

There is infinite energy available in the universe which we can use to bring desired changes by clearing and polishing our lattice grid, which is connected to our nervous system.

Ashwin

Chapter 9

The Best way to Predict the Future is to Create It

It was now time to make Abir a shepherd out of a sheep . . . and many more like him.

Today was the day of the destiny child.

Both Abir and I had reached the radio station of Sector 34, much before time. Sitting in the green room, I went through the last minute preparations for the battle royal that was coming up.

The sky was cast again and the only visible thing outside was darkness. But I was sure that care for human race would win over the wrathful temper of the approaching storm, as I was holding the sun in my hand.

"War-game planning makes one tense," I could imagine a grey-haired general saying so. Although I was not a general and certainly not grey-haired, but the scope of my canvas was as important, differing only in the fact that I was fighting the game of mind.

I was reminded of my distant aunt, twice removed from my mother's side, who had a rotund figure, who used chaffing as a winning tool as against my another not-so-distant aunt, just once removed, who used a dough pin as her fighting tool against my rather subdued uncle, who called her 'a dashing young lady'. Having watched both the ladies in action from close quarters, I wanted to become a 'dashing young man' and wanted to knock the enemy over with a dough pin, quite like Obelix does. But the situation being different in this case, I had the dual responsibility of wearing the general's hat as well as fighting on the front like a sepoy. So I chose to ignore my aunt once removed in favour of my aunt twice removed.

I had prepared efficiently throughout the week like a lawyer. There were times when a cold, unseen 'what if' surge would touch my mind with an icy finger, but I shooed those thoughts away.

It was six in the evening. Abir walked up to me with a boy holding a tray by his side. Abir was looking much more confident today. It was a kind of walk in which the mind-steps seemed to be matching the physical ones.

"*Guruji*, all set?" Abir asked in a chirpy voice.

I just nodded as I was too preoccupied.

Pointing towards the cake and coffee in the tray, Abir said, "Manvi has sent these for us with her compliments. She has conveyed that it will take another half an hour."

"*Panditji*? Where is he? He hasn't reached yet," I asked.

"About to be here in five minutes," Abir replied looking at his watch.

"Good." I heaved a sigh of relief.

"Let's have coffee before we go," I said. Abir nodded in approval.

"I practiced KLT in the morning," he announced happily.

I did not reply but gave him a confident look, a look which a rum-soaked warrior on the front would give to his fellow men.

The door of the green room screeched, announcing the arrival of the *panditji*, the so called messenger of *the destinies*. He was wearing a crisp white *kurta* and *pajamas*. His girth had increased by a few inches and so did the number of rings with different coloured stones. If I remembered correctly, the *tikka* on his forehead had changed colours from red to turmeric yellow now.

"Maybe the change was in accordance with some shift in planets," I thought and smiled.

We wished *Panditji*. It was good to see Abir not touching the feet of *Panditji*. I smiled again.

Suddenly, my phone buzzed. 'Manvi', the name flashing on the screen furnished my inner self with a delightsome pleasantness. She had called up to ask if we were ready.

Within a few minutes, Manvi came to us. She escorted us to the recording studio. After crossing a corridor of about thirty yards, she stopped in front of a big, shining wooden double door. The security guard opened it for us. It was a considerably spacious room with a glass partition. On the other side of the room was a soundproof cabin that had all the paraphernalia of radio-recording like mixers, microphones, amplifiers, digital studio telephones, and a few cabinets.

Manvi briefed us about the format of the programme and the handling of the equipment. She then helped us to settle down in our respective seats. As we wore our headphones, *Panditji* looked a little lost because of the incongruence of the environment.

"All set?" Manvi enquired.

We all said, 'yes' but *Panditji* was pretty loud. Perhaps he didn't realise that he was wearing headphones.

'ON AIR' began to glow. The man sitting on the audio-mixer shouted, "One, two, three, start."

The sweet and silky voice of Manvi filled the studio.

"Good evening, Chandigarh. Today, I am going to take you to heaven. Book your tickets now." Her words were followed by her loud giggle.

It was a treat to watch her the way she connected to her audience and introduced the issue of the day.

"Today's episode is unique as we try to explore the true potential of astrology from a scientific viewpoint. In our panel we have the learned astrologer *Panditji* Anand Sharma of Astro Visions. He has more than thirty years of experience in helping people repair their fortunes. Even his father *Pandit* Suresh Sharma was a well-known astrologer of our beautiful city. Welcome to the show, *Panditji*."

"*Namaskar!*" *Panditji* folded his hands and continued, "Thank you, Manvi."

"Then we have Mr Ashwin, a pass-out from our very own Punjab Engineering College and University Business School, Chandigarh, and now a successful corporate executive. Surprisingly, a spiritual mind with a radical distinction, who has promised to help us transcend beyond skies where we will be assigned extraordinary powers to create our own destiny. He will tell us how. No need to be surprised. Don't you all believe me? Then listen to a man of otherwise a few words. I said 'otherwise' because today he is going to talk a lot to all of us," Manvi went on.

I marvelled at her energy and vibrancy on mike.

"Hello, Mr Ashwin. Welcome on behalf of our listeners," she echoed again.

"Hello, everybody," I said.

I was a little nervous. The stakes were high, very high. I took a deep breath to calm down.

"And this is Mr Abir, a devotee of astrology or should I say of *Panditji*." Manvi smiled as she introduced Abir and continued, "Apparently he is a victim of the planetary play."

"Hello!" Abir said.

Manvi carried on, "And the last participant is you, my dear listeners. Please dial in for your queries. We'll be taking your calls as they come," she said and announced the phone number as she turned towards *Panditji*.

"*Panditji*, my first question is to you. What is astrology?" Manvi set the ball rolling.

He was taken aback with the simplicity of the question while I smiled as I was happy with this opening gambit.

Suspecting the unsuspected, *Panditji* was cautious in his reply. "It is the study of the influence that distant stars and planets have on one's life. We study the various combinations, ascendants, *dashas,* and transits to predict one's future."

Panditji paused and looked at me for assurance.

I nodded and asked, "*Panditji*, why do you think astrology today is not held in high esteem? I know Sir Isaac Newton was also a great astrologer. But where have those golden days of astrology gone?"

Panditji thought for a moment and replied, "See, it is not astrology that has lost its esteem. It is some charlatans who are masquerading as astrologers. After learning a bit, they get bitten by the bug of earning quick money and start selling their half-baked knowledge. The advent of computers has brought calculations within everybody's reach. Even if they get a few predictions right, their popularity among the select few grows exponentially."

"Well said, *Panditji*, I wish all these dealers of faith were as honest," I appreciated. His facial expressions instantly wore an attitudinal grin as an effect of my compliment.

I continued in support of my 'running with the deer and hunting with the hound theory', which I reckoned was a perfect fit for the moment. "Yes, I agree. Science's rejection of astrology is based on ignorance, the science's ignorance. Do you know when the astronomer Edmond Halley asked Sir Isaac Newton how he could possibly believe in astrology, he answered, 'Because I have studied the matter, sir. You have not'."

I could see admiration in the eyes of the audience around. Abir liked my policy of non-confrontational 'running with the deer' phase. But the hound in me came pouncing back as I delivered the coup de grâce, "Even Shakespeare made comments in his epic novels about 'stars influencing our lives'. But sorry to say, astrology is about the planets of our solar system, not the stars."

Panditji moved his tongue on his now dry lips as he shifted in his chair. I had him nervous, at least to some extent.

After a few moments, he found his tongue again, "There are other reasons also. There is a lack of talent in this field. Most people learn it as an add-on specialisation and not as first choice. There is hardly any new research in this field. Many times the results are faulty because people do not even know the correct time of their birth."

Manvi was more than excited as she was continuously enjoying the feedback from the editor that the TRPs were rising.

The studio phone started ringing.

"Excuse me, our first caller is on the line," Manvi silenced us by placing her finger on her lips.

"Hi, this is Kanwal from Chandigarh. Sir, can you please tell me something about *Rahu*? My astrologer has told me that my seventh house is afflicted by *Rahu* and my next few years will be dominated by bad times. I am really worried about this," the first caller addressed us.

"One more of our kinds," Abir blurted so spontaneously that both Manvi and me couldn't help smile.

Panditji could feel the impulse of instant fame. He looked visibly inflated as he started imparting his knowledge about the suns and moons and their galaxies. "Well, it is said that *Rahu* is the dragon head of a demon who was detected by the sun and the moon and was killed by Lord Vishnu, while drinking nectar. Since the demon had drunk some portion of nectar, he became immortal. He is known to have swallowed the sun in vengeance," *Panditji* explained and looked at Manvi.

"Why are you so afraid of *Rahu*, Kanwal?" I quizzed as I winked at Elfy sitting on my left shoulder.

"Because my *Panditji* says so. *Rahu* is a demon because of whom my life has plunged into a struggling chaos," the caller sounded quite worried.

"Even Abir's *Rahu* has created similar chaos in his life. Am I right, Abir?" Manvi looked at Abir and asked him.

"Yes, I cannot get married for four more years because my moon is seventh from *Rahu* and its period is going on," Abir replied glumly.

"Abir, do you think all our problems are caused by *Rahu*?" The caller was a little more confident this time. Maybe because he had found a co-sufferer in *Rahu*.

"*Panditji* says so," Abir replied robot-like. *Panditji*'s chest swelled up by a couple of inches on hearing this.

I took out a pen from my pocket, picked up a notepad, and drew two overlapping circles. Manvi was delivering a live commentary on what I was doing.

"Astronomically, the moon in its orbit on a northerly course crosses the apparent path of the sun. This point of intersection is known as *Rahu*. The fact that solar eclipse occurs when the sun is at *Rahu*'s point is explained in stories as the swallowing of the sun by *Rahu*," I clarified.

"So what do you want to convey?" Manvi asked.

"Elementary. The ancient Hindu observers of the sky were aware of the cause of solar eclipse and so described the process in the language of metaphor. *Rahu* is just an astronomical point in the sky," I concluded.

There was pin-drop silence in the studio as everyone reeled under the impact of my words.

"This makes me feel better sir. Thank you!" the caller said after a while and hung up.

Manvi thanked Kanwal for calling and addressed her audience again, "Isn't it amazing, listeners. You can call if you find yourself in any such kind of dilemma in life."

It was interesting to see that not only the radio-listeners but the editor and the assistants sitting in the studio room were listening to us with rapt attention.

"Folks, the next caller is here with us," Manvi's excited voice resounded.

"Good evening, Manvi. This is Mehak here," the caller said.

"Hi, Mehak. How are you? What would you like to ask?" Manvi spoke to her as if speaking to a very dear friend.

"Firstly, I would like to tell Mr Ashwin that it's actually an eye-opener, the way you are putting astrology in such a different perspective altogether," the caller said.

"Thanks, Mehak," I responded.

"Your question, Mehak?" Manvi asked.

"My astrologer has predicted something similar and I am very scared about it. I mean I feel so helpless at the hands of destiny," she expressed her concern.

"The highest frequency of our universe is that of love. The fear of such dominating negativities has led to a resultant decrease in the overall positivity in this world. It is the time for awakening. It is the time for empowerment," my words personified conviction.

"But what do I do? I want to get rid of this fear." Mehak's restlessness for the solution was well evident from her tone.

I replied, "You are scared because your mind has picked up the thought given to you by your astrologer and has started believing in it." I continued, "Our thoughts determine our present and future of what is contained in our lives. It's all about our choices. We will attract or draw the responses and results to wishes and thoughts, from the universe exactly according to how and what we choose."

"This means the fear is the result of my thought?" Mehak had an amazing calm in her voice this time as she thanked me.

Phone calls were pouring in. Manvi had another caller on the line.

"*Panditji*, what are these weekly predictions? Are these true?" the caller asked. I looked at Abir and smiled because he always used to read those and plan his week accordingly.

Panditji replied, "There is a group of twelve zodiac constellations from Aries to Pisces that make a ring around the earth called the ecliptic and is the path the sun and the moon both appear to take around the earth. This imaginary band is what governs many an individual's personality traits."

He paused as if to gauge my feedback. I was listening very attentively to him. This was a cue for him to carry on. I was keeping my aunt twice removed, who was desperate to speak, in a listening mode.

Panditji's fountainhead of information continued. "A combination of four elements of fire, earth, air, and water in each sign signifies a certain type of personality trait."

"Could you give me an example, *Panditji*?" Abir asked. He always needed an example to understand the concept.

"For example you are a Capricorn which is an earth sign. So, it is associated with action in the material world," *Panditji* replied to Abir and continued pointing at me. "In your case, since you were born on December 14, you are a Sagittarian, which makes you a clear thinker and a wanderer."

"But I am no longer a Sagittarian, *Panditji*," I countered.

"How can you say that?" *Panditji* was offensively defensive.

I opened my iPad and showed him the picture of the imaginary zodiac he had just talked about. Abir was poring over my neck as I started explaining, "The twelve zodiac signs were created nearly 3,000 years ago. Due to the changes in the alignment of earth's position all these years, a new sign has come in. Now we have thirteen zodiac signs and most of the original signs have slipped up by almost a month."

As I was explaining, Manvi delineated the details of the site to the listeners.

"So?" Abir had his mouth open now.

"So, once this effect is factored in, your zodiac sign may have changed. You, for example, are no longer a Capricornion but a Sagittarian!" I announced and winked. "You have been reading the wrong horoscope all these years."

"But how come some of the predictions mentioned in the weekly columns were coming true?" the caller on hold questioned again.

"Very simple. As I told Mehak, we pick up that thought and transfer it to the universe and it responds exactly the way we think. Am I clear?" I clarified.

"Thank you, Ashwin. I really thank you for this piece of information." He hung up after pouring out his gratitude.

Abir clapped, which showed he was breaking free from the demons within him.

"You should be awarded a PhD degree," complimented Manvi.

I replied modestly, "I hardly qualify."

The next caller was coming through.

"I am an astrologer this side," an elderly voice boomed.

"May I have your name, sir?" Manvi asked.

"What's there in the name?" He seemed quite seasoned.

He stated, "You believe that astrology is a science. Please prove it. Your generation loves to challenge the old value system and the ancient tried and tested theories. I'll be happy if you prove them wrong."

The new caller had brought two divergent feelings in *Panditji*. One that of support, and the other that of competition.

Panditji replied emphatically, "Since astrology is based on a system of calculations, it is very scientific. In the olden times astronomy and astrology were studied together. Most of the great mathematicians, scientists, and physicists were great astrologers too. The accomplished ones were called *Trikal darshee,* who could see the past, present, and future."

"That's right, *Panditji*. Yes, astrology appears in truth as any other science, if interpreted and applied correctly," I added, with a stress on 'if'.

"What exactly do you mean? How does it work?" the anonymous caller fired a volley of questions.

I replied, "See, in science, hypotheses are made and observations are done many times and a resulting theorem or principle is formed forever. Astrology currently lacks that kind of experimental backing."

Panditji's neck moved in agreement as I explained further, "In case of medical science also, the doctors can go wrong in diagnosis. Even accounting for human error, since medicine is a science, probability of getting predictions correct is very high. Most importantly, doctors have many types of equipments to back them. See, a scan can seldom go wrong because it shows the internal conditions of the body."

"Yes, you are right. Lack of backing by scientific instruments leaves us open to confirmatory tests," moaned *Panditji*.

"And see, even without this kind of support, we are doing well to help the ones in misery," the caller almost announced his victory.

"And if I am able to provide you scientific instruments which could back your astrological findings?" I delivered my master stroke just at the right time. The reaction had to be seen to be believed.

Abir, who had been a silent listener till now, tried to get up from his seat but the wires of headphones prevented him from doing so. He tried to say something, it would have been a 'wow' I believe, but nothing audible came out. *Panditji* began rocking his chair.

"How?" *Panditji* was the first one to recover as Abir began a slow descent towards his chair.

"That's an interesting 'how'! I would like to add on another 'how' on behalf of our listeners," Manvi jingled again.

I smiled, as a beautiful reason had been added on to prove this 'how'.

I experienced immense satisfaction, which showed on my face. I became more relaxed, arms folded, lips pulled in a kind of sheepish grin, quite unlike that of a vanquisher, eyes askance.

"We will come back to the instrument shortly. Let me first explain to our learned caller some scientific basis of how astrology works.

I shifted my attention back to the caller and asked, "First tell me, what kind of details do you ask from your client before you make any predictions?"

"Well, that's simple. Time, place, and date of birth," the caller replied.

"What is the significance of these details?" I asked.

"So that we can draw the horoscope of the client as per that time and position," he answered in a matter-of-fact manner.

"What time do you consider is the right time for making a horoscope?" I queried further.

He hesitated in replying and then said after a while, "Whatever the client tells us."

I smiled. I had him where I wanted him to be. I opened my iPad, turned towards Manvi and Abir, and started a slide show. Manvi, like a perfect anchor, kept divulging all the details to the listeners about the happenings in the studio.

I said, "Think that our solar system is an atom with the sun at the centre. As you know, Abir, when an electron joins an atom, an atom's properties change. It is same with the sun."

At the mention of his name Abir gave a nod, almost making poor *Panditji* also do the same, whether he understood it or not.

I continued with the next slide. "Every moment the sun receives charges from various planets like Jupiter, Venus, Saturn or Mars, the solar winds then carry these patterns and deposit them on the earth's grid. The earth has its own magnetic field, due to its magnetic iron nickel core, which receives the constantly changing patterns, what the astrologers call transits, and delivers them to us humans. The grid pattern continuously changes and acts as a communication engine for human DNA."

"But I don't see any correlation of all this with astrology," the caller asked.

"Let me explain," I continued, "Human DNA is sensitive to magnetic field. At the moment of the first breath, the baby's lattice takes on the energetic imprint of the earth's magnetic system by induction. Able and genuine astrologers, like our *Panditji*, know this." I pointed towards *Panditji*. "This personal human lattice permanently holds the life's programming in form of an astrological chart with the baby's first breath."

The anonymous astrologer hung up as only a beep responded to Manvi's address to the caller.

"Awesome," Abir applauded. "Since everything is pre-programmed, we cannot change anything?" he asked.

I replied, "Although your future comes pre-programmed, you can still change your future by creating it."

Abir had a confused look on his face again.

I paused, as I wanted him to apply his mind. Slowly I hinted, "Remember, Abir, there is energy available in the universe . . ."

"And we can get that extra bit of energy in our system which is necessary to bring about the desired changes," Abir interrupted in excitement.

"Not extra but infinite energy," I said and carried on, "Our lattice is so important in everything we do. It is our present communication system as it is directly connected to our nervous system. Clearing and polishing this grid and aligning our intention physically allows for better communication with the DNA and the cells. By focused energising, we can clear old belief systems and negative behaviour."

The time had come to open the case and to give our listeners physical demonstration of things I had been talking about.

"What is this radiance around the head of the deities in their pictures, *Panditji*?" I asked.

"It is the positive energy of the deity. It signifies their divinity. It shows that they are the messengers of God," *Panditji* replied.

"Since this light can actually be seen, this implies that this energy is matter." I had a childlike enthusiasm in my voice.

"If you say so," *Panditji* did not understand science but did not want to acknowledge so.

"*Panditji*, this circular divine light is nothing but aura. Our great Vyasa Maharishi understood that matters possess energy and he called these energies as *Prana Shakti* and *Parma Jyoti*. Later, our famous scientist Sir Einstein also used similar concept in establishing correlation between mass and energy."

As I started with the demonstration, rendering verisimilitude to her narrative, Manvi started the live commentary in her beautiful tinkling voice. I set up the compact machine on the table and asked *Panditji* to give me his saliva sample which I inserted in the machine. I then asked him to move around in that room.

To his utter surprise, the machine always pointed in his direction wherever he went.

"How is this happening?" Panditji, not a bold seer anymore, asked in amazement. His eyes were wide open, almost in a trance.

Before I could speak up, Abir replied, "Your frequency is locked in this machine. It will follow you wherever you go."

I was happy, very happy to see him so sure and in teaching mode to a person who had been running or ruining, take your pick, his life until then.

"That was a game changer. At least one mind has changed. That's me," Manvi echoed again.

"Make that two," Abir announced his independence.

"Exercise number two coming up now, friends. Will you remove all the stones from your fingers and put them aside," I said.

"Why?" *Panditji* asked meekly, removing his more than half a dozen rings and putting them away.

"See, *Panditji*, most of the celebrities, politicians, and the commoners wear stones suggested by you or by your elk. Why do you suggest them stones?" I asked.

"Well, gemstones bring peace, good health, or any desired achievement of goals to the wearer," replied *Panditji*.

"Well, well, we have another caller." Manvi spoke to the person on line. He was a businessman.

"Sir, do you think these gemstones can help me grow my business?" he asked.

"Good question. Two things are to be considered here. One, whether your horoscope has been analysed and secondly, whether the astrologer is charging the right value for his product. More often than not, the fear of the gullible customer is capitalised as these guys perform special *puja*, ostensibly as a cover up for high charges," I spoke in a raised voice and looked at Abir, who was now busy taking off the rings from his fingers.

"Sir, do you think these astrologers dupe us for earning few bucks?"

I replied, "This machine will take care of the analysis part. It will scan your body and suggest which gemstone suits you the best. But I tell you, there are a few genuine people also in this profession, like our *Panditji*."

Panditji's tense muscles relaxed and everybody could see that. In the next five minutes, I matched *Panditji*'s aura system against the master samples and gave him a list of stones he needed to wear. The list matched whatever his horoscope pointed at. As a conclusive test, I even measured his aura without and with gemstones.

By the end of the experiment, I was like a tribal king. My kinsmen, *Panditji* and Abir, were almost ready to worship me. But since this was no jungle and since I was not a tribal king, nothing of this sort happened. It would not be unreasonable to say that my stocks had risen steeply.

"Now, here comes the answer to your question regarding your progress in business. Gems can actually collect, focus, and electro magnate energy. Each stone has its own influence, function, and vibration. Importantly, gemstones with their powerful energies and profound resonance with the human body may also serve as a perfect tool to enhance your confidence level that boosts your business, health, and relationships," I concluded.

Just then, Manvi announced that there was another caller on the line.

"This is Ashima. First, I would like to tell you that you guys are doing a great job. I am impressed, really."

"Thanks," I sounded modest.

"I have a couple of questions, Mr Ashwin. You mentioned that one's life is programmed into one's DNA structure at the time of the first breath. The first question is that if the life is programmed, can we actually forecast events which are going to happen in one's lifetime?"

I replied, "Ashima, see, the horoscope's software is derived from the resultant of frequencies of the sun and various planets on the human body at the time when the baby takes the first breath as he or she comes to the world."

"How do we know about the impact of these frequencies?" Ashima's question clearly indicated her curiosity to know the details.

I decided to unfold a fact that was very close to my heart. I had not shared it even with Abir or Manvi.

I said, "I have actually started working on a machine called Frequency Forecast Metre. Once you feed individual specific inputs into this metre, it will be able to calculate the impact of various frequencies on one's body and would be able to forecast the events that are going to happen second by second. It will take a couple of years to accomplish this."

Abir and Manvi both looked at me in amazement. I smiled.

"Oh, that's something unbelievable! Some revolution! This is so enlightening."

Abir and Manvi didn't say anything but their looks said it all.

"My second question is, how can we create our own future? I mean how do we actually do it?" Ashima's young and sweet voice chirruped again.

I looked at my watch and then at Manvi and replied, "Ashima, I would love to explain the whole thing but we are running short of time and the programme has to end now."

Ashima shot back, "There are many more who would love to listen to you now. Can't you do something?"

I looked at Manvi who looked at the editor in return. The TRP ratings had gone up significantly. The editor signalled Manvi to carry on as they were getting reports that almost half of Chandigarh had tuned in to our programme by now.

Manvi came back on air and said, "Folks, the compelling demand of our listeners is forcing us to continue. So, now, ladies and gentlemen we are in for a maa . . . aaa . . . gic, the magic of Kasauli Lights Technique."

Then began the action-packed half of the programme, the most awaited moment of my life. I had not only the opportunity to awaken people but to empower them too. *The true impact of the old gypsy lady's fourth riddle was coming to life.*

Since we had time with us now, I began my story with my visit to the gypsy lady in Mexico. Manvi, intermittently joined the storytelling. In order to make things more interesting, she read out the four riddles and asked the listeners if they could solve them.

Manvi spoke in an excited voice, "We are putting these riddles on our web site. We have special rewards for anyone who cracks them first."

The calls came in thick and fast. It was getting rather difficult to connect to all the calls because the queue had got long. Almost everybody had his own version to tell. The younger generation had especially tuned in. More and more people were tuning in as we got circulated on the social media, where the riddles were being discussed.

As I reached the point where I had to teach the Kasauli Lights Technique, I requested Manvi not to take any further calls for at least the next fifteen minutes to avoid disturbance.

There was a pin-drop silence in the radio station as I asked the audience to take three deep breaths. As if the angels were on watch, the clouds had cleared up, and all those who could see were eagerly watching the lights of Kasauli. People, whether they were on rooftops or in parks or in cars, were all glued to the faraway lights. For the next ten minutes, as I took them through the complete process of Kasauli Lights Technique, the listeners lived their dreams in their minds. I took special care to teach them the 'power of transformation'. My voice was choked as I explained the conversion of the devilish *Rahu* into a lovable Elfy.

"And yes, friends . . . the best way to predict the future is to create it," I said and wrapped up my presentation.

There was a long silence when I finished my presentation. Manvi took a few seconds to realise this, as she continued to stare at my face before breaking into a slow applause.

"Wow! Wasn't that something!" She addressed her listeners and continued, "Drop us your feedback at our email . . . " And she gave the email id and went on with her anchoring jargons.

She then thanked us all and the listeners before going off air.

She gave me a big hug as soon as she got free. "Splendid returns," I thought.

The editor came running in and said, "Great job, Ashwin. Manvi, that was awesome. Can we serialise this?"

Manvi looked at me and waited for my reply. Just then her phone rang. I could see the name of Samar flashing on the screen of her phone. She moved aside to take his call.

I looked around the studio and saw *Panditji* sitting in his chair with drooping shoulders. I walked up to him, took an envelope out of my pocket, and handed it over to him.

He looked at me curiously without speaking.

I said, "*Panditji*, this contains a business plan which combines the usage of the frequency-measuring machine with astrological findings. You will see that you make a lot more by guiding people right."

"Right? What do you mean?" he asked.

I put my hand on his shoulder and said, "Yes. *Panditji,* astrology is a wonderful tool to be used as a guide for improvement. You are not just predicting future but creating destinies. Such is your power. Whatever you feed in people's mind, they will reverberate on that frequency. They will think accordingly and their thought processes will shape their lives. Instead of feeding fear, feed positivity. That's all I ask for."

Panditji nodded and took the envelope.

Abir came and embraced me. He admitted, "I am back to Kabir. Thank you, brother. Let us go to the bar and plan my wedding details and celebrate. I will ask Manvi if she can join us."

His face had the peace of being without chains. I was happy for him.

Abir moved away to speak to Manvi who was still busy on the phone. I watched from the corner of my eye that there was that special smile on her face which a woman has when she loves to be where she is.

My heart was choked and my eyes a little moist. Poor Elfy, who had been my constant company, also had droopy looks on his face. Like me, he had understood that perhaps, the lord hath taken her away. He came close to my ear and whispered, "Let's change the future by creating it."

"No, Elfy. Not in this case. No egoism, if not being loved by my beloved. I let go off my desires," I replied with a heavy heart.

Time stood still as she trespassed into an alternate world of mind. Tears rolled down her cheeks as Kasauli lights provided her all the answers she desired. She knew exactly what her heart wanted, what every part of her being craved for, what her soul yearned for.

About Manvi

Chapter 10

She Is Mine

It was just a few days after the radio chat show. Samar had invited Manvi to cover an international seminar on alternate healing. As she reached the auditorium in Sector 22, she could see Samar waiting near the entrance.

"Manvi, you are late. I have been waiting for you since eight." Samar's anxiety was inexplicable to Manvi.

"Waiting? For me?" Manvi asked, raising her brow.

"Yes, for you," he reverted back to his polite and sweet usual self.

She continued to look at him with a question in her eyes.

"Manvi, may I request you to inaugurate today's programme," he and his eyes, both pleaded.

"Me? But why?" Her surprise was as genuine as her expression.

He replied, "In fact, I am supposed to inaugurate it, but I feel that I am more of a host than a guest." Suddenly, a solemnity shrouded him as he continued, "If Priya was here, I wouldn't have bothered you."

"Priya?" Manvi had heard this name for the first time.

"She was my wife," he replied. Visibly, a wave of gloom took over the bloom of his face.

Manvi didn't know how to respond. But she did not want to be the cause of delay for this wonderful seminar either. Her well-bred dilemma gave in to a generous helping of compassion. She approached the pink satin ribbon and inaugurated the seminar amidst a clapping crowd and bunches of flowers.

Reverend Mother Christina, the chief speaker from the USA, was on a mission to bring awareness about the concept of alternate healing. With a calm, composed, and glowing face, she looked no less than an angel as she talked about the maladies created in our bodies due to our hidden complexes, twisted psyches, and self-created sorrows. According to her, each one of us has the power to heal, not only our bodies but also our minds, sorrows, circumstances, and relationships, thereby creating a future of our choice.

Manvi felt that the lecture was an encore to my 'Kasauli Lights' philosophy. She was too engrossed to realise when the four hours' session got over. She rubbed her eyes softly and came back to her material self, wondering at the divine scheme of things. She happened to have had this unique experience twice within a week's span, first through me and now through Samar.

"I am feeling good and that's what is important," she thought and smiled. She was happy to have sensed that emotion after a long time.

As Manvi was about to move out, a group of people thronged her to congratulate her on the success of the chat show. They talked very fondly about Ashwin and his theories.

"I am doing KLT twice a day. It's very helpful," one of them remarked excitingly.

Manvi couldn't help a smile as she thanked them. Samar wanted her to join his staff and guests for a cup of coffee but she sneaked away quietly as she knew that she had gathered quite enough, to feel and write.

On her way back, she dialled my number. She wanted to share her day's experience with me.

"Hi, Ashwin, how are you?" she asked.

"Hi," I replied in a reserved voice.

Manvi could feel that my voice was denied of spirit as I made no further effort to break the silence that followed.

"Ashwin, today I had an amazing experience," she swooned.

"What happened?" My voice was still sans cheer.

She then proceeded to give a detailed account of the last few hours of bliss she had been through.

She concluded, "After today's seminar, I am very clear in my mind that I am going to transform my negative energies into positive by serving fellow beings through alternate healing. I had learnt this art some time back but I think the time to practice has arrived now."

"Sounding serious. But that's great," I said cheerfully.

"I will, however, need your and Samar's constant motivation," she said.

"Always at your service," I promised with mixed feelings.

As soon as she reached home, Manvi narrated the same story to her mom.

"I am feeling very light and excited," she said as she hugged her mother.

"Oh! I am so happy for you. It was great of Samar to have made you the guest of honour," Mom said, holding her daughter in a warm embrace.

Manvi went for shower as her mom was mulling the thought of Manvi taking Priya's place. Just then, the doorbell rang and her happy steps proceeded to the door.

It was Kabir at the door, with a card and a box of sweets in his hands.

"*Namaste, Aunty*, I am Professor Kabir Sharma. Is Manvi home?" Kabir introduced himself and asked.

"Kabir? Oh, you were on the chat show with her. No?" she asked.

"Yes, I was. I have come here to invite Manvi to my wedding," Kabir replied.

"Congratulations, *beta*! Come in. I'll just call her," Manvi's mom said as she escorted him to the living room.

It was a very tastefully done-up house. After making him sit, Manvi's mom went inside. She brought him a glass of water and said, "You people did a wonderful job on the chat show. Mr Ashwin was too good. Is he a scientist or what?" she asked.

Kabir chuckled and said, "He is actually a friend. We were together in college."

"Oh! I thought he was some elderly gentleman. I mean the way he was talking, he sounded so mature, so experienced!" she exclaimed.

"You are right. He is great in genius, noble at heart and all graces as a human. A gem of a person, truly," Kabir replied, seizing his opportunity.

"Not only that. You know, *Aunty*, he has achieved so much at such a young age. He earns well, has travelled around the world, and is such a loving son and a caring friend." Kabir wanted to add, *And he loves your daughter.*

"Hi, Kabir." Manvi entered the room.

"Hello, Manvi! Looking nice and fresh," Kabir complimented.

"Oh really? Thanks," her reply was more of a bubbly chirrup.

Kabir got up and handed over his wedding card to Manvi and said, "I am getting married on December 23 at Kasauli. It's a destination wedding."

"Oh wow! That's wonderful. Ashwin's efforts have borne fruit, finally. I am so happy for both of you," she said excitingly as she gave him a big hug and asked him for a coffee.

Kabir smiled and nodded a 'yes'. He had never seen this chirpy Manvi earlier.

As she left to make coffee, her mom spoke in a little sombre tone, "Why don't you people insist her on making up her mind for marriage. I am worried about her."

"I think if there's a good match, why wouldn't she say yes?" Kabir replied.

"Good match? Kabir, there's a wonderful match." She got a little excited and secretive when she said so. With a glitter in her eyes, she asked him, "Has Manvi ever told you about Samar Taneja?"

Without giving any time for Kabir to reply, she continued, "What a boy he is! He is everything that I would dream for Manvi. So successful in life and above all, a good human being." She was gazing in infinity as she talked about Samar.

Kabir almost had a sinking feeling for me as he could clearly see how impressed she was with Samar.

He thought for a while and said, "*Aunty*, actually you are right. But I think we need to keep in mind that she has already faced many hardships. She needs someone very mature, who would understand her and care for her. Without any doubt, Samar is a rich man, but does Manvi like him . . . ?" Before Kabir could say more, Manvi was back with coffee.

He was pleasantly surprised to see Manvi in a very different mood that day. She was glowing and smiling, as if the ghost of her past had been exorcised.

Manvi's mom took her daughter's hand in hers, looked into her eyes, and asked, "Manvi, do you like Samar?"

Kabir, who was about to sip his coffee, suddenly froze.

To her own surprise, Manvi did not flee away from the situation this time. She thought about the day's happenings, about Samar's caring nature, and most importantly, she thought about bringing a smile to her mom's face.

She looked at her mother and said, "He is a great guy."

Her mom heaved a big sigh of relief. Kabir felt sad for me, but he felt genuinely happy for the change in Manvi. He sat with her for almost an hour discussing the wedding plans.

***

As far as material gains were concerned, I had been visualising all fine things in life and they were manifesting one by one in my life. I had got my black E-class Mercedes just before Diwali.

"Wow! That's wonderful. I will bring my *doli* in your car," Kabir exclaimed on the phone and excitingly carried on, "You have to teach me this art of thinking and growing rich after my honeymoon is over. Okay?"

"But you already know," I replied.

"I want you to push me into it," Kabir said adamantly like a child.

"Okay, dumbo, I will. In fact, I would love to broadcast this during our next chat show," I replied.

"But then everyone will become rich!" Kabir exclaimed like a child again.

"Not only rich, we'll empower people to create a utopian society. This is the true essence of the gypsy's last riddle," I replied.

Kabir was silent for a moment before he said, "All right, Ashwin, do it your way. But Manvi and I need a treat for the car. Okay?"

"Roger," I said and hung up.

I had a strange sense of satisfaction as I slid my hand on the car. As if I had become Samar's equal. I hated myself for this feeling. I still had a long way to go to achieve what *Guru* Jetchi expected of me. I looked over my left shoulder. Elfy was smiling.

***

The charm of the small, sleepy but intoxicating and mysterious hilly town of Kasauli had borrowed furtherance from Kabir's delight. He had chosen Kasauli as a destination for his wedding, as it had been a ceaseless favourite of ours since college days. He had booked the pristine Kasauli club for three days.

The wedding was just a day away now. Kabir was finding it too hard to resist his impulses to share his excitement with whoever came his way. Cheers and laughter had found a perpetual refuge on his face. He was leaving no stone unturned to make sure that all the guests had an enjoyable stay.

"It's four o'clock. Where are these buggers?" He cursed restlessly while walking towards the gate as he waited desperately for Ashwin and his other friends.

He shivered as the town had begun clothing itself in the freeze. But soon a glow marked his face as he saw me walking down towards him from the parking, which was exactly opposite the entrance of the club.

"Hi, Ashwin," he shouted as we both picked up pace. A false annoyance accompanied the friendly abuses and chiding as Kabir complained of my delayed arrival.

"There were customers from South Africa and . . . " I said but Kabir didn't let me complete.

"You will never change," he boxed me while saying so.

"All set for the knot?" I asked.

"Jitters," Kabir murmured.

"What jitters? Be a man and get ready to enjoy the forbidden fruit. And you were so eager to taste it. Now when you are in for it, why get nervous?" I teased him.

"Yes . . ." Taking a deep breath he winked at me and asked, "And what about you?"

"Me?" I smiled and faked surprise.

"Yes, you. If Manvi . . ." Before he could finish, one of his uncles came our way. He looked at him and said, "I believe you have some guests waiting for you in the lounge."

Kabir requested his uncle to show me Room number 16 as he walked away towards the lounge.

Room number 16 turned out to be a beautiful and welcoming two-room cottage. A typical hill-town suite with a fireplace in the sitting room. I had my hands in pockets and a smile on my lips. The place looked awesome. All the minute details had been taken care of. The tidy and aesthetically done-up cottage, with Victorian set-up, was absolutely apt for Kasauli and its weather. I switched on the lamps. The room got drenched in a soft and warm glow. The bedroom was equally inviting, nice and cosy. My appreciation could not go on, as a knock at the door distracted me. It was Kabir.

He said, "Look who's here!"

"Manvi!" The name flowed spontaneously.

She looked so cute with a twinkle in her innocent eyes. But just then, the inevitable happened. The moment she entered the room, she tripped as the edge of the carpet interfered with her stiletto heels. Rather than helping her, both Kabir and I burst into a hearty laugh. She was nothing but embarrassment personified.

"Idiots, you are of no help," she shouted, all the while trying to balance herself.

"Manvi, a leopardess can't change her spots. No?" I stated as I was testimony to her charming clumsy side. I remembered the sight at the airport and in *Panditji*'s office. I extended my hand to her as Kabir tried to straighten the corner of the carpet.

As her hand slipped into mine, she suddenly went quiet and she followed me to the sofa.

"Are you okay, Manvi?" Kabir sounded concerned.

She smiled and said, "Yes, I am. But I don't know how it happened."

"How it happened! Ask why it happens," I exclaimed and laughed.

"Am I that clumsy?" Manvi's childlike tone filled my whole being with a charmed passion.

Kabir excused himself to arrange for tea while I went to the washroom. He would capitalise on every moment wherein he could push Manvi my way. Manvi got up and went up to the window. It was around five in the evening. Hills were surrendering to the dusk. Their very magnanimous being was dissolving bit by bit in shadows.

Manvi looked at the door of the bedroom from where Ashwin had gone in. Then again she looked outside. Her soul was calm today. Her mind was experiencing an unsaid and unheard peace.

"What are you doing near the window? Close it. It's too cold to leave it open," I said as I came back to the sitting area and rushed towards the window to help Manvi close it. It was breezy, and the short, lacy sleeves of her white top were fluttering in rhythmic motion. She tried to cover herself with a colourful warm stole as she moved towards the sofa.

Manvi rested her head on the back of the sofa and closed her eyes.

"Are you tired?" I asked her.

She shook her head. As I saw her reclining, I was wondering if it was fatigue?

"After a long time I am breathing. It's so peaceful here," she was talking to herself.

I looked at Manvi and thought, "Everything is here under this roof. The comforts of an undisturbed recluse, a beautiful uninterrupted winter evening, and Manvi. How perfect! What else can I ask for? All is so well with the world."

My thoughts were halted by the knock at the door again. It was Kabir with a waiter carrying a tray.

"So silent? You guys must be tired," Kabir's excited tone echoed.

"Tea! Great. I think it is required to beat the chill," Manvi spoke in a welcoming tone.

All three of us talked and laughed and pulled Kabir's leg about his wedding, over sips of tea. After a while Manvi raised herself Saying, "Okay guys, now I need to get ready for the evening."

She again went to the window and looked out at the swaying pines, the twinkling lights on the hills near and far, and the wandering vapours of the fog. Then she turned and looked towards the warm cosy ambience of the room with me sitting by the fireplace. She closed her eyes as if she wanted to store this view in her eyes forever.

"Come on, guys, hurry up. Be in the club in half an hour," Kabir shouted.

"Half an hour? What do you mean? I need more time," Manvi reinforced as she walked away.

I looked at Kabir and smiled to indicate my compliance with her.

I reached the club hall at 8 p.m. A combination of foggy winter skies and the decorative lighting made the club look heavenly. The hall was filled with the rustle of silks and furs, the giggles of the ladies, and the tinkling of glasses. It was *Ladies' Sangeet* evening. A perfect host, Kabir was busy looking after the guests.

I was slightly uneasy as Manvi was nowhere to be seen. I lifted my eyes from the watch, looked at the entrance, and breathed easier. Manvi was making her way in. She was holding her *lehenga* from one side below the waist and walking cautiously. I advanced towards her but had to stop midway.

She had been ambushed.

"Hi Manvi!" Samar spoke with a large grin on his face. Manvi looked around and saw him.

"Samar?" Manvi asked in surprise.

"Yes, Samar," he said, fluttering his eyes.

"When did you come?" Manvi asked.

"Just landed." His charming smile lit up his face, like always.

"Great," she said, and her attention shifted to her attire again. Perhaps, she was cautious so as to avoid any expected mishaps like tripping.

"You are looking like a doll," Samar said softly.

"Hmmm . . . thanks," she replied.

Pointing at her hand with which she was holding her *lehenga,* Samar said, "May I?"

"Samar, I am fine," Manvi tried to discourage him, knowing his mannerisms quite well. I was watching all this from a distance. Not being able to tolerate it, I tried to get lost in a drink.

Ceremonies of the *Ladies' Sangeet* had begun. Singing, dancing, and cocktails followed a small *puja*. Manvi mingled with a few people, spoke to Kabir's mom, and headed towards me where I was standing by the side of fireplace, with a drink in my hand.

"Ashwin, you don't sing or dance?" Manvi looked at me and asked.

Indifferent to her question, I asked with a slight authority in my tone, "Where were you?"

Before we could proceed with our conversation, a sound on mike grabbed our attention. It was Samar.

"Ladies and gentleman, I think there are two most blissful things God blessed us with. Music and women and I always give way to both." As he announced this, his charming smile was quite visible in the well-lit cosy hall. Amidst a loud laughter, he held the piano accordion and requested for everybody's attention.

"Friends, I dedicate this to the girl I care for the most, the girl I like the most." The crowd hooted as he announced and looked towards Manvi and said softly, "And the girl I can die for."

I could see the colour of Manvi's face changing as she tried to look at me faking an unsuccessful pretence of not acknowledging the words of Samar.

The deep seductive sound of the instrument suddenly filled the hall.

"He's good," Manvi uttered as if trying to behave normally.

"He is," I reinforced.

Samar was looking extremely handsome in a blue blazer as he played the instrument with so much dexterity. All eyes were focused on him, some in awe, some in jealousy. The audience was spellbound with his excellent performance. There was a loud applause as he bowed stylishly after finishing the rendition.

He walked towards us. I suddenly realised that Manvi had disappeared by that time.

"That was a great performance, Samar," I complimented him, shaking his hand.

"Thank you, Ashwin. It's good to see you again," he greeted me in his usual lively fashion.

"I hope the girl you can die for, is equally good," I said with a probing smile.

He raised his arms theatrically and swooned. "Oh! She is wonderful."

I hailed a passing waiter and fixed a glass of scotch for him.

"Cheers!" Our glasses clinked as we toasted Kabir's wedding.

"Where has Manvi gone?" he asked me as he took a big sip.

"She was here. Don't know where she rushed off to," I replied, looking around.

Two pairs of eyes X-rayed the room but couldn't spot her. Just then there was a loud *dhol* beat at the entrance as a group of ladies entered in a line to perform the traditional *jago* ceremony. Leading the pack, with an earthen pot over her head, was Manvi.

Jago is a traditional Punjabi pre-wedding ceremony and is intended to wake up friends and family to rejoice and dance together in celebration. A pot is decorated with candles and carried on the head whilst dancing and singing folk songs.

It was heartening to see such a big change in Manvi. She seemed to have shed her past inhibitions and looked like she was beginning to enjoy life again. I was very happy for her. Dressed in a chic and colourful red *lehnga* and golden *choli*, Manvi looked resplendent. They soon started going around the hall making all dance to the rhythmic drumbeats. The party had reached its zenith.

I noticed that Manvi was not well clad and it was getting increasingly cold. I fixed up a vodka for her and walked towards her.

"You need this," I said standing behind her, watching her slender back. Her *choli* was almost backless and it was hard to control my feelings. I could have stood there for hours admiring her lovely back, more intoxicating than the drink in my hand.

She turned around, gave me a big smile, took the glass, and said, "Thank you."

Just then Samar arrived, took her hand, and pulled her towards the dance floor.

"This number is dedicated to Kabir and Sabeeha. All couples please join us." It was Samar on the mike again. The lights were dimmed, and the band switched on to slow rhythmic ballroom music. The first couple was on the stage and a few more joined in.

Manvi was in his arms. His right hand was resting on her beautiful bare waist. I watched in agony till the song lasted. I looked at her face which did not betray any emotions. I found refuge in the elixir in my glass.

It was about eleven when we finished dinner and walked back to our cottages. The chill pierced through our bones as we walked back. Perhaps the hills sleep early. The town was sleeping but the twinkle of the lights seemed to be guarding the hills under the shelter of the dark roof. Our teeth were clattering and puffy clouds escaped from our mouths. I could see Manvi shivering. I took off my coat and wrapped it around her without seeking her permission. She looked at me and said nothing. I felt ecstatic at the mere touch of her hand. I wished she felt the same.

"Let us have coffee," Kabir offered. He was holding Sabeeha's hand.

"Oh yes!" Samar echoed.

"Let us go to my cottage. We have all the arrangements there," Kabir said.

Kabir's cottage was just a ridge above mine. We all trooped in. I headed to put on the fire, Kabir and Sabeeha went to the kitchen, Manvi went towards the window to have a view of the valley below, Samar squatted on the sofa, and Nidhi sat on the chair. Nidhi was Kabir's cousin and had been following Samar ever since she saw him perform. She seemed smitten by him and apparently Samar was quite used to such female interest. He still looked immaculate, not a hair out of place.

"Hot coffee," Sabeeha announced as she entered, the now warm room. Kabir followed, carrying a tray in his hand. Cupping the mug of steaming hot coffee felt good.

"So, Kabir, what does your astrology say? Who is going to be the boss of the house out of the two of you?" Manvi asked, chuckling.

Kabir grinned from ear to ear and said, "Obviously Sabeeha. Even Ashwin's compatibility test will support this." He looked at me and winked.

"What?" Manvi raised her brow and asked.

"Their compatibility. We can measure it." My matter-of-fact attitude in making that statement was inversely proportional to their curiosity. Sips of coffee lost their charm suddenly.

"You mean you are going to measure the quantity of their love and care for each other?" Nidhi asked in a tone that clearly indicated that it was something incredulous.

"That's boo. No science can do that," Samar said. His doubts indicated clearly that he found this certainty, an allusion.

"Yes, I can. Anybody with a torch?" I said, taking up the challenge.

"Yes, there is one in the pantry," Kabir replied as he walked towards the pantry. He got the torch, and we both went out to my car. We came back shivering, five minutes later, with a black briefcase in hand.

Tapping my briefcase, I smiled and said, "Pandora's box".

Everybody came close to me. Samar left his sofa and grounded himself, literally.

I asked Kabir to write Sabeeha's name and give it to me. The woolly fold of the glowing room warmed up even further and silence descended. I took out the instrument and spent two minutes on explaining its working. They all looked at each other in wild surmise, as I proceeded to complete the test.

As soon as the test finished, I remarked, "Wow! Great compatibility. Made for each other."

Sabeeha fluttered her long eyelashes, as a polite recognition. Kabir wrapped an arm around her shoulder.

Manvi was spellbound. Though she had seen this instrument during the radio show, yet the compatibility test was a discovery for her too.

"If we market this properly, we can make millions from this instrument," Samar spoke in an excited voice..

"I know you can. But I intend to use this instrument for increasing universal love as it has several such usages," I replied.

Samar kept quiet for a while and then said, "Ashwin, will you do this test again? This time for us."

"Us?" My response was a little dramatic.

"Yes, us." He looked behind him where Manvi was sitting and attested his answer.

"Yes, us. Me and Manvi," he repeated.

"Me?" Manvi, a far cry from the soft-spoken Shakespearean lady, cried out.

"Why me?" she reiterated.

"Ashwin, let's see what the instrument comes out with," Samar insisted.

"What rubbish. Stop joking, Samar." Manvi tried her best not to acknowledge the seriousness of Samar's offer. "It's just a compatibility check, girl," Samar assured her. She shrugged her shoulders as if it was nonsensical.

I picked up the frequency measuring instrument. My hands shivered. 'It had never felt so heavy,' I wondered why. I had to make an effort, both to hold it and to smile as I looked at Manvi. It was no less than a 'last look'.

Amidst the bated breaths, throbbing hearts and skeptical minds, I began writing the most difficult test of my life. It wasn't their test, but mine. Abir looked towards the ceiling as if in prayer. And Elfy, with his eyes bigger than ever, froze on my shoulder. I had never seen him so scared. The process began and within minutes got over. But those few minutes were long, very long.

The results were breathtaking. 'Perhaps, Samar aspired better,' I thought as I nervously announced, "They have passed and passed in flying colours."

Abir was transfixed and Elfy listless.

In no time Samar took off his solitaire, went down on his knees, and proposed to Manvi, "Will you marry me?"

Manvi, dumbfounded, tried to speak with great difficulty, "Samar, this is really funny."

Before she could physically react, he held her hand and slipped the ring onto her finger. I could see the colour of her face changing from pink to red. Not knowing what to do, she took out the ring, put it on the table, and walked out of the room. Samar followed her. Nidhi followed Samar.

Kabir came to me and expressed his annoyance, "Why did you do their compatibility test, Ashwin?"

"Why, what's wrong?" I asked, taking off my cravat. The room had become quite warm.

"You love her so much," Kabir said in a low voice.

I turned towards him, held him by his shoulders and looking right into his eyes, I said, "Kabir, my love is above and beyond any instrument. The power of love is above every damn power, frequency, or thing."

"But, Ashwin . . ." He wanted to say something but I cut him short.

"Relax and go to sleep. Tomorrow is a big day for you. Gear up for that," I said and winked at him.

He was still frowning as I left the room.

As I walked out of Kabir's room, my eyes met with nothing but mist. I tried to look hard through the haze but the lights on the hill were not visible. Perhaps the mist would take time to clear away….

The next morning, Kasauli hills woke up to a celebration. Kabir, all decked up, along with his contoured assemblage of women adorned in bright orange, red, and pink silks, and men in tweeds and stripes, gleamed upon the site of the day.

But I couldn't feel the touch of the sighing winter breeze, smell of the perfumes, hear the music, see the morning rays struggling with the fog or taste the dewy vapours, the heart being not too happy.

"Hi, Ashwin," Manvi whispered in her soft voice.

My wit went into boots.

"Where are you?" She clicked her fingers, "Are you all right?"

"Yes, I am," I could barely speak. She was looking pretty with angelic innocence in her eyes.

"Kabir is looking for me," I replied as I made an excuse and walked away.

The day went by. Wedding ceremonies went on till evening. Samar left no stone unturned to flatter Manvi. Whether it was taking care of her food, her comfort, or going overboard with compliments, he did everything possible under the sun. Though feeling awkward, his sophistry and innocent ways of wooing abated Manvi from getting annoyed.

Today's Manvi was far different from the Manvi of yesterday. Lost in her own thoughts, she walked out of the hall to take a walk in club lawns. She was trying to get in touch with her inner self.

Kabir was seeing off his guests as he noticed Manvi standing at a distance. He quietly approached her and stood by her side, his arms folded.

"It's chilly here, Manvi," he said.

Manvi turned towards him. Tears were rolling down her cheeks. Kabir gently hugged her and asked, "What's wrong, Manvi?"

She took a deep breath, wiped her tears, and said, "Samar wants me to marry him."

Kabir kept quiet. "Is he serious?" He asked after a while.

"Yes. He proposed again today," she said.

"Be happy then. He is an eligible bachelor," Kabir replied.

"I don't want any bruises again," she mumbled with her eyes cast down. Kabir waited for a moment. He took her hand and walked a few paces towards left. He stopped and looked up the hill. Manvi followed his gaze and saw the Kasauli lights, which were trying hard to liven up the dense darkness.

Kabir said, "Clear your mind of the ghosts of your past and the dilemmas of your present. And you know how? The way I cleared out the clutter of false notions from my mind."

Kabir patted her shoulder gently and walked away.

Manvi took a long soulful look at the Kasauli lights, closed her eyes and took a deep breath, oblivious of the cold she was breathing in. Something silenced all her nerves and awakened all her senses. The soul of hers was on a journey to fetch for her what she always wanted. Time stood still for her as she trespassed into an alternate world of mind. There was a storehouse of her wishes, she just had to pick.

"Oh!" She uttered even in this blissful state and tears started rolling down her cheeks. As she slowly opened her eyes, a piercing chill shook her from top to bottom. She looked at her watch and realised that she had been standing there for about thirty minutes.

She was still relishing the immense serenity that she had been craving for a long time and it manifested on her face in the form of a calm confidence. She started walking back to her room but the steps were no more weary. Kasauli lights had provided her all the answers she had desired. She knew exactly what her heart wanted, what every part of her being craved for, what her soul yearned for.

She went back to her cottage with a smile on her lips. She showered and changed, humming all the time. Smelling like a fresh flower, she walked out.

Her footsteps were in sync with her heart. Her heart's very firstling instinct navigated her towards the neighbouring door. No cord, no cable, still she was drawn. Eyes were in the need of satiation, for the very first time.

"Why so?" Now she had the answer to this thought. She had found her universe right next door. She barely knocked. With the mere touch of her hand, the door opened.

"Are you there?" she called softly.

"Come on in."

The words were very simple but they sounded as if she had been longing to hear them for ages. She stepped into the room. I was reclining on my bed, reading. I had my glasses on, as I usually did, when I had to read. I looked up and smiled. Draped in a scarlet red *sari*, with a pearly waistband, loose curls hanging on her shoulders, she walked in with a mild tinkle of her anklets.

Sitting in the bed, I extended my hand. She looked at me with her kohl-adorned dreamy eyes, and her henna-embellished hand held mine. I held her and made her sit by my side. She had reached where she belonged. She brought her face close to my chest. She dissolved in me as if she had been a part of my very being for many lives. Her eyes were closed and I was looking at her face.

"You are me," she whispered.

"Yes," I replied as if we had been talking to each other since eternity.

"You are me," she repeated as if to quench her thirst.

"Hmmmm . . . " I caressed her hair.

She looked up. Before her lips could speak something, her eyes whispered, "I am yours, only yours."

I looked over my left shoulder. Little Elfy, with his eyes covered with his hands, was jumping up and down with joy.

As I raised my eyes, the sight across the foggy window pane was so fair, so touching. Lights of Kasauli flickered behind the breezy pines as if they were in haste to leave me with my most fancied dream. "Your destiny child has grown up dad," I whispered to myself.

I extended my arm and switched off the light. I turned slightly and embraced my life in my arms and whispered in her ear, "My soul. My soulmate. You are mine. Only mine."

Authors' Profile

Vinny Ajrawat

Dimpy Ajrawat

CEO of an Export House, Vinny is an alumunus of Punjab Engineering College and University Business School, Panjab University, Chandigarh with a strong academic excellence and inclination towards performing arts. The restless passion to give tongue to his experiences, coming from vast international travelling, sought its way to the creation of Kasauli Lights

An English Language Consultant with British Council and Oxford University Press and a Reiki healer, for Dimpy various degrees in English language were surely the instruments but the execution of the dream called Kasauli Lights needed none other than an intense desire and a c h i l d h o o d r e v e r i e t o connect with her fellow humans to feel, what they feel.

Both of them have ventured into the literary world of word pictures through their debut novel Kasauli Lights. Being progeny of the Defence background, they inherit the spirit to fight for the tribe of humans, walk the untrodden and flirt with the mystery of luscious landscapes. Hailing from as variant backgrounds as Science and English language respectively, both Vinny and Dimpy leave discernible imprints of the same on their work.

Glossary

1. Rahu - Rahu is one of the <u>navagrahas</u> (nine planets) in <u>Vedic astrology</u> and is paired with <u>Ketu</u>.
2. Panditji-priest
3. Hola (Spanish)-hello!
4. Como Estas(Spanish)-how are you
5. Te amo(Spanish)- I love you
6. Golgappas-Indian snack taken with spicy sweet and sour juice
7. Dekkho -take a look
8. Banjaras-Indian gypsies/ nomads
9. Ghaghra Cholis-colorful ethnic Indian skirts and tops
10. Atrapadas- a Mexican game, played by kids
11. Peepal-peepal tree
12. Chai- tea
13. Jyotish Acharya-astrologer
14. Salwar Kameez- Indian dress
15. Dupatta- scarf or stoll
16. Namaste- traditional Indian way of greeting with folded hands
17. Kurta Pajama-traditinal Indian dress worn by men
18. Mauli- sacred thread worn on wrist by Hindus during religious ceremonies
19. Rudraksh Mala - Sanskrit: *rudrākṣa* ("Rudra's eyes"), is a large evergreen broad-leaved tree whose seed is traditionally used for prayer beads in Hinduism. The seed is used in the making of a bead chain or *mala*.
20. Maha Dasha- major period

21. Kundali- horoscope
22. Asura-demon
23. Shri Rahu Maharaj- His highness Mr Rahu
24. Tikka- a coloured spot worn by Hindus on forehead
25. Upaay – astrological solution
26. Samosa- a spicy Indian snack with potato stuffing
27. Masala scenes – spicy scenes
28. Oye- call out
29. Tappa- the action of a ball touching the ground to bounce back
30. Bada Khana- a function where Army personnel of all ranks of a formation feast together
31. Yaar-buddy
32. Shani - Saturn
33. Chowk-square
34. Gulabjamuns- Delicious sweets in the shape of dark brown balls made out of flour and milk powder
35. Bhai- Brother
36. Parathas- (In Indian cookery) a flat, thick piece of unleavened bread fried on a griddle.
37. Egg Bhurji- instant dish made out of squashed eggs
38. Ketu- according to Vedic Astrology, Ketu is a planet
39. Pallu - long trailing part of a *saree* or a *dupatta* that can be draped around and across the shoulders
40. Puja- worship/Religious ceremony
41. Ji – the word used as a mark of respect while addressing the elders
42. Beta- son
43. Gulal- red coloured powder used to smear one another while playing Holi
44. Kamarband - waist band
45. Jhanjhars- anklets

46. Holi –an Indian festival celebrated by playing with colours
47. Moksha- salvation
48. Tandoor- earthen oven
49. Guruji – teacher (generally religious)
50. Churidaar- well fitted tights
51. Elfy – a pleasant imaginary figure in miniature human form
52. Padmasna- it's a lotus position in which you sit during Yoga.
53. Dhaba- roadside crude restaurant
54. Perfecto- Okay
55. Trikal Darshee – one who can foresee and predict future
56. Aunty- a colloquial term used for aunt
57. Doli-palanquin
58. Lehenga-traditinal Indian long skirt
59. Ladies' Sangeet- a pre wedding ceremony where friends and relatives sing, dance and party together
60. Dhol- drum
61. Jago- pre marriage ceremony in Punjabi weddings where people sing and dance together